DERIB + JOB

W9-AMB-991

YAKARI

AND THE GRIZZLY

9th CINEBOOK
The 9th Art Publisher

Original title : Yakari et le grizzly

Original edition: © LE LOMBARD / DARGAUD 1978, by DERIB & JOB
www.lelombard.com

English translation: © 2006 Cinebook Ltd

Translator: Erica Jeffrey
Lettering and Text layout: Info Elec sarl
Printed in Spain by Just colour Graphic

This edition first published in Great Britain in 2006 by
CINEBOOK Ltd
PO Box 293, 18 John Dutton Way
Ashford, Kent
TN23 9AD
www.cinebook.co.uk

A CIP catalogue record for this book
is available from the British Library

ISBN-13: 978-1-905460-16-8
ISBN-10: 1-905460-16-3

9th CINEBOOK
The 9th Art Publisher

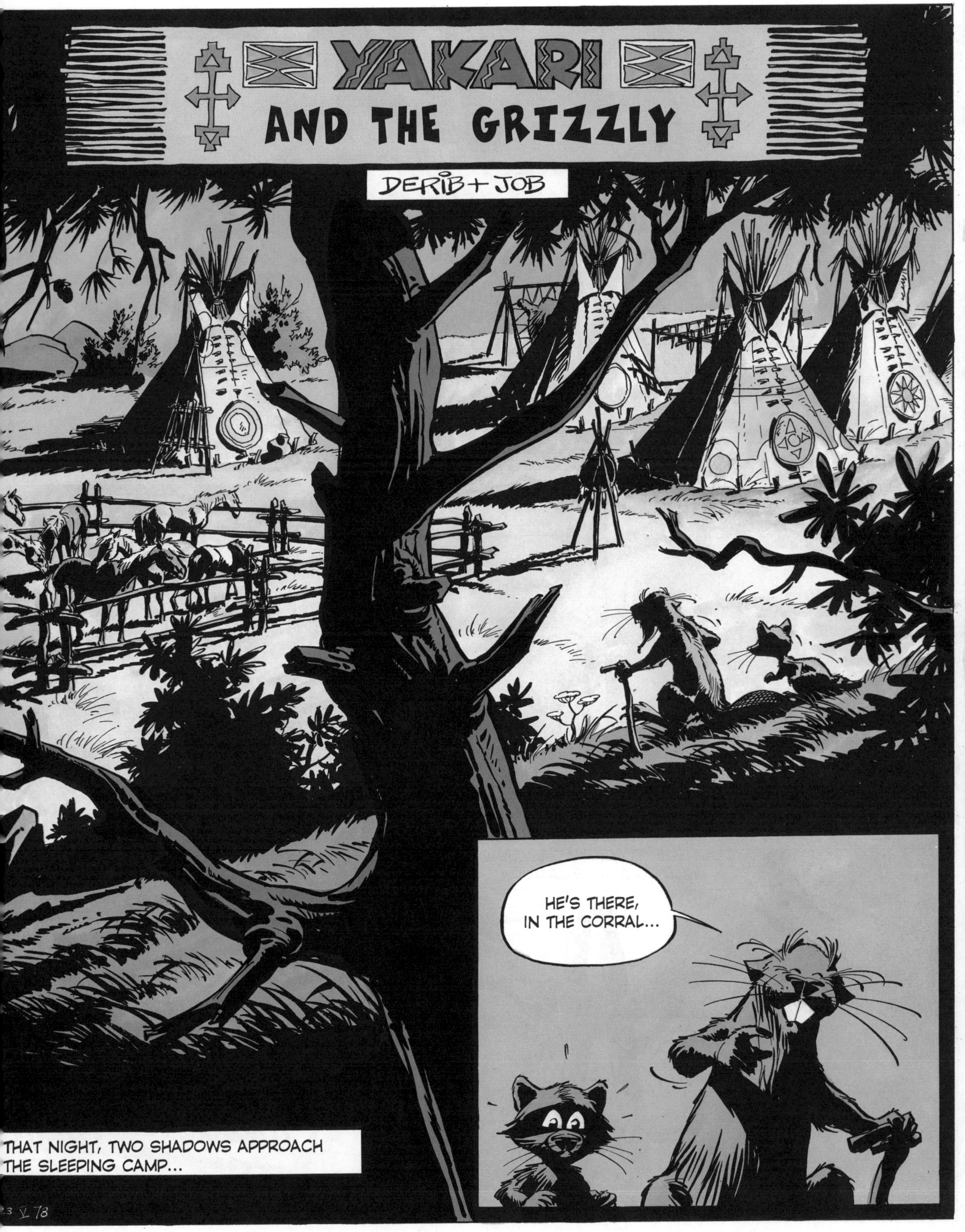
YAKARI
AND THE GRIZZLY
DERIB + JOB
THAT NIGHT, TWO SHADOWS APPROACH THE SLEEPING CAMP...
HE'S THERE, IN THE CORRAL...

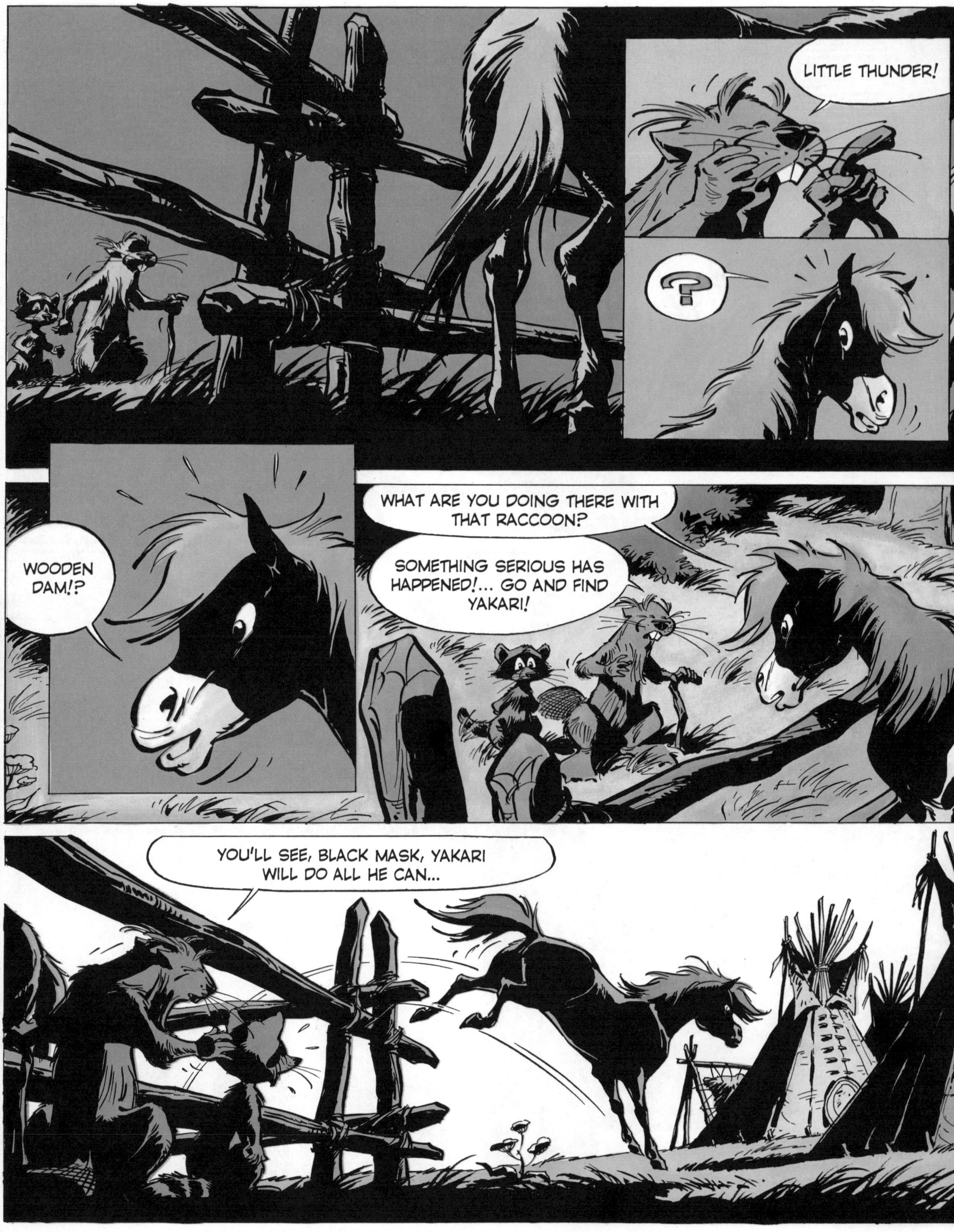
LITTLE THUNDER!
?
WOODEN DAM!?
WHAT ARE YOU DOING THERE WITH THAT RACCOON?
SOMETHING SERIOUS HAS HAPPENED!... GO AND FIND YAKARI!
YOU'LL SEE, BLACK MASK, YAKARI WILL DO ALL HE CAN...

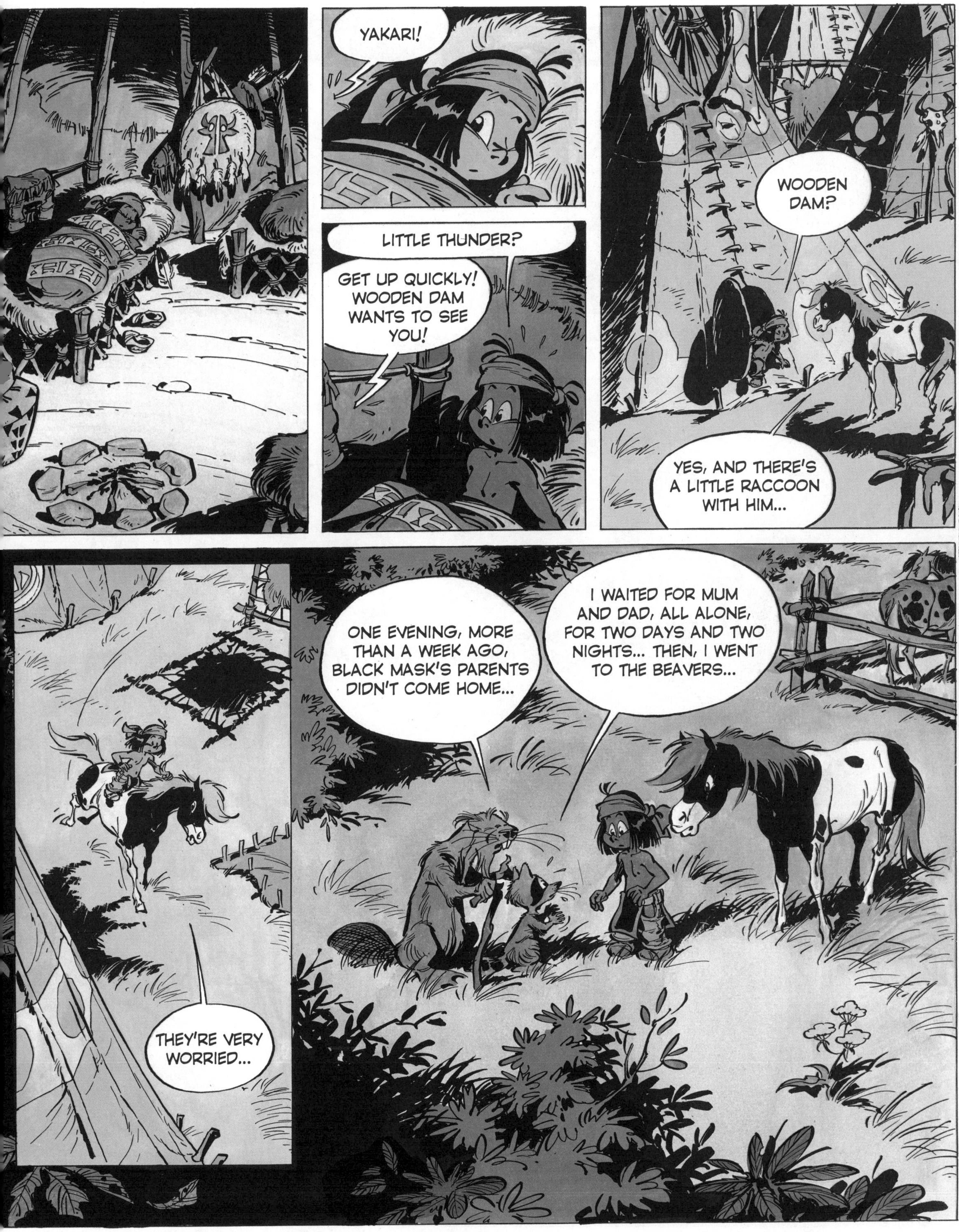
YAKARI!
LITTLE THUNDER?
GET UP QUICKLY! WOODEN DAM WANTS TO SEE YOU!
WOODEN DAM?
YES, AND THERE'S A LITTLE RACCOON WITH HIM...
THEY'RE VERY WORRIED...
ONE EVENING, MORE THAN A WEEK AGO, BLACK MASK'S PARENTS DIDN'T COME HOME...
I WAITED FOR MUM AND DAD, ALL ALONE, FOR TWO DAYS AND TWO NIGHTS... THEN, I WENT TO THE BEAVERS...

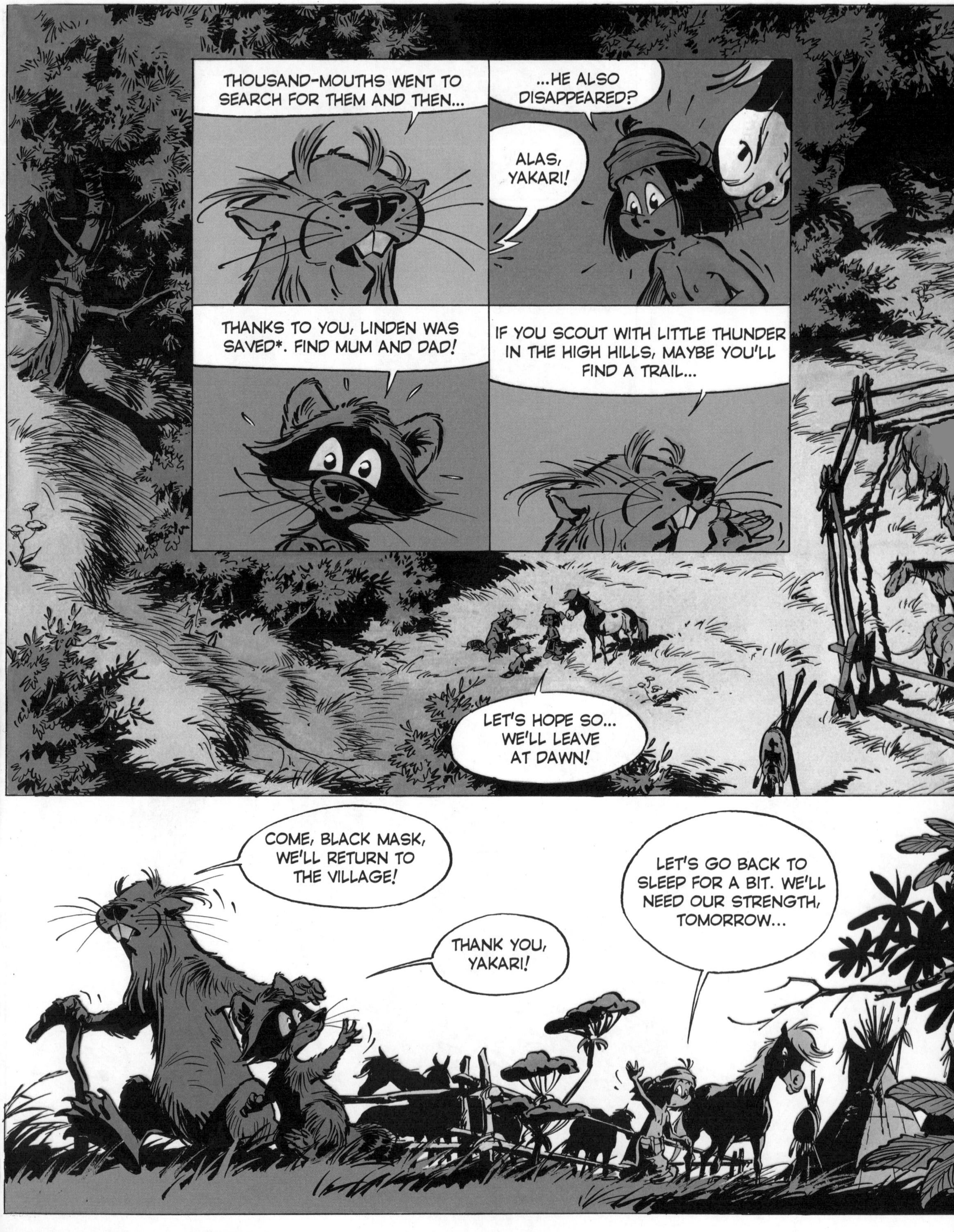
THOUSAND-MOUTHS WENT TO SEARCH FOR THEM AND THEN...
...HE ALSO DISAPPEARED?
ALAS, YAKARI!
THANKS TO YOU, LINDEN WAS SAVED*. FIND MUM AND DAD!
IF YOU SCOUT WITH LITTLE THUNDER IN THE HIGH HILLS, MAYBE YOU'LL FIND A TRAIL...
LET'S HOPE SO... WE'LL LEAVE AT DAWN!
COME, BLACK MASK, WE'LL RETURN TO THE VILLAGE!
THANK YOU, YAKARI!
LET'S GO BACK TO SLEEP FOR A BIT. WE'LL NEED OUR STRENGTH, TOMORROW...

*SEE "YAKARI AND THE BEAVERS"

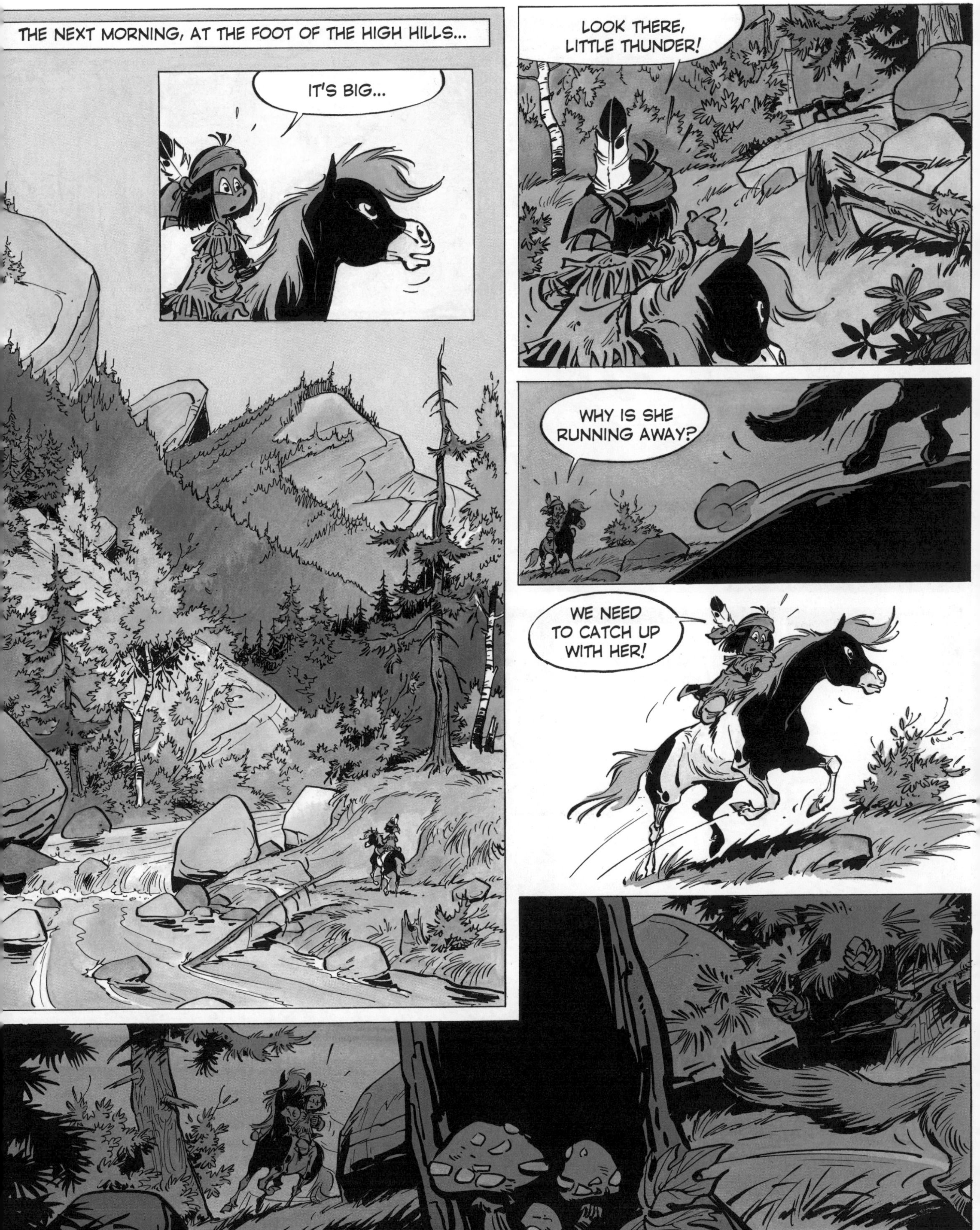
THE NEXT MORNING, AT THE FOOT OF THE HIGH HILLS...
IT'S BIG...
LOOK THERE, LITTLE THUNDER!
WHY IS SHE RUNNING AWAY?
WE NEED TO CATCH UP WITH HER!

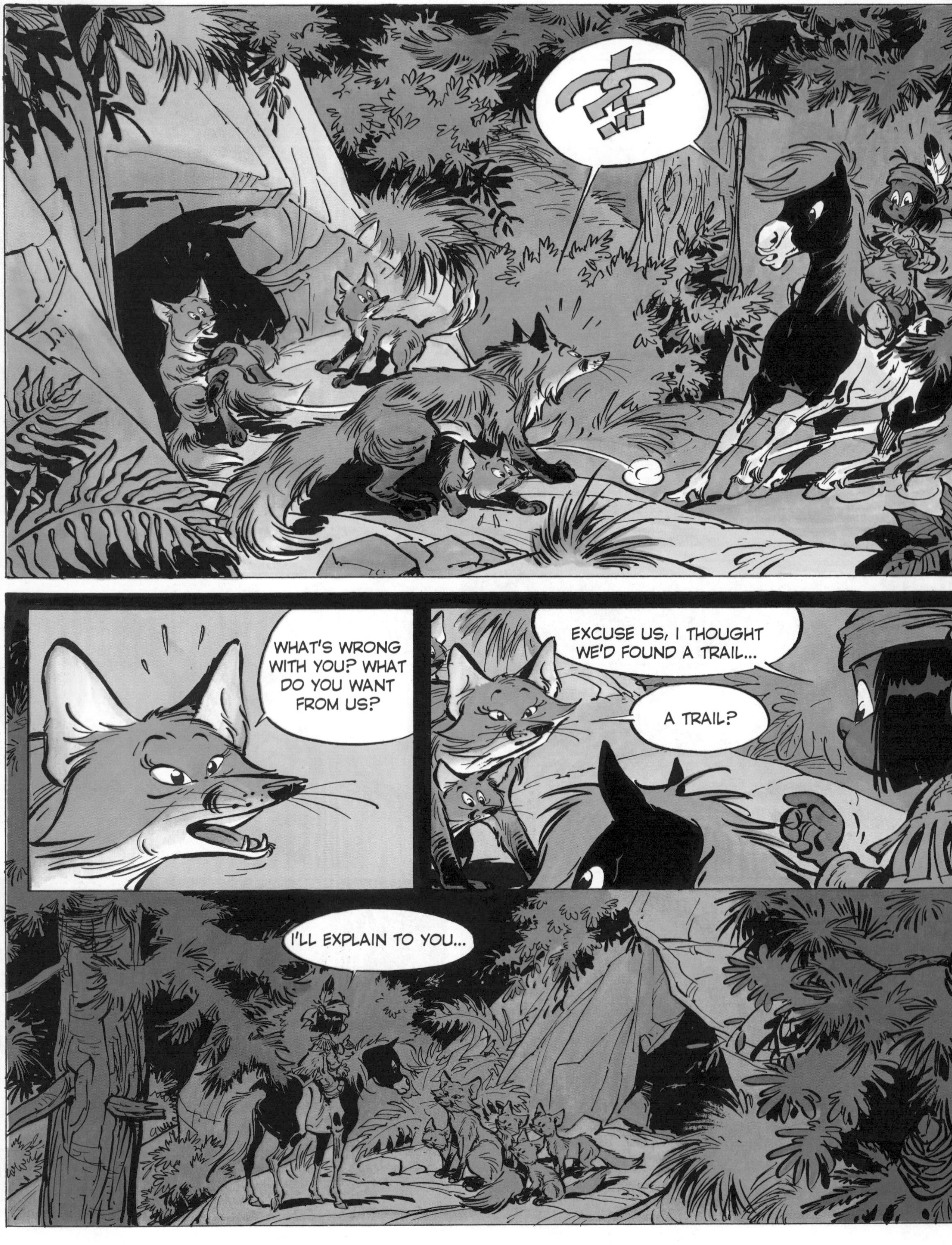

?!?!
WHAT'S WRONG WITH YOU? WHAT DO YOU WANT FROM US?
EXCUSE US, I THOUGHT WE'D FOUND A TRAIL...
A TRAIL?
I'LL EXPLAIN TO YOU...

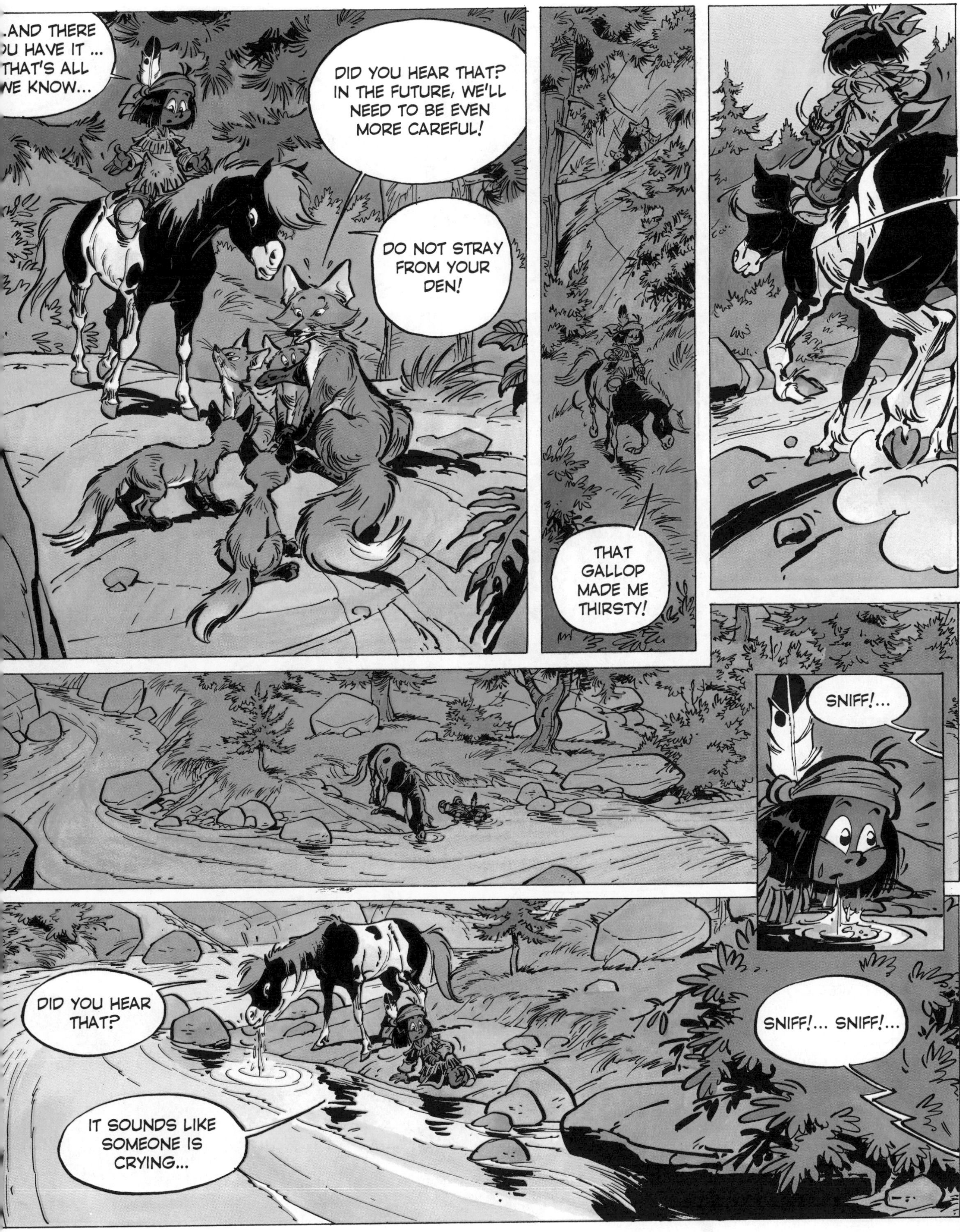
.AND THERE
DU HAVE IT ...
THAT'S ALL
WE KNOW...
DID YOU HEAR THAT? IN THE FUTURE, WE'LL NEED TO BE EVEN MORE CAREFUL!
DO NOT STRAY FROM YOUR DEN!
THAT GALLOP MADE ME THIRSTY!
SNIFF!...
DID YOU HEAR THAT?
SNIFF!... SNIFF!...
IT SOUNDS LIKE SOMEONE IS CRYING...

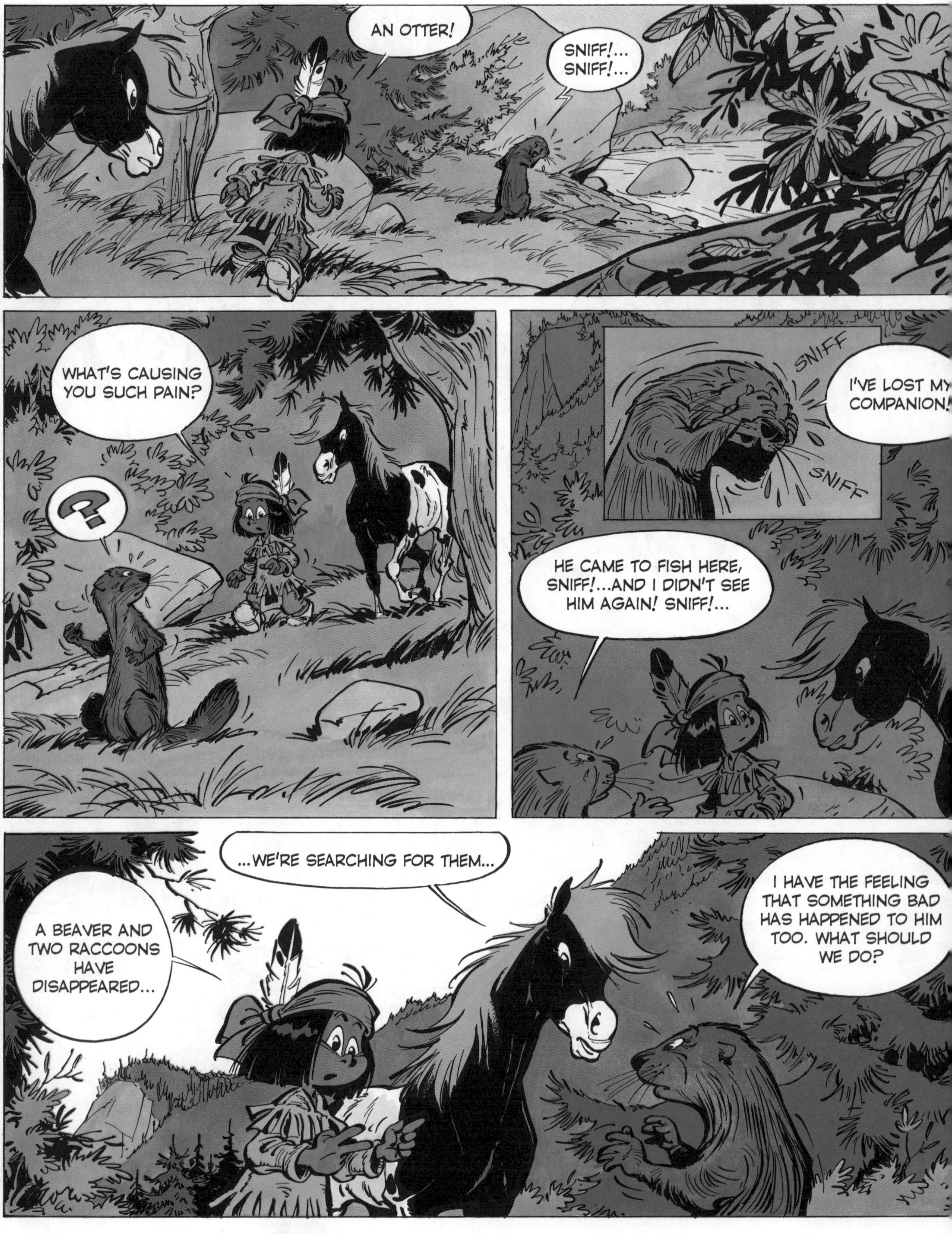
AN OTTER!
SNIFF!... SNIFF!...
WHAT'S CAUSING YOU SUCH PAIN?
SNIFF
I'VE LOST MY COMPANION!
SNIFF
HE CAME TO FISH HERE, SNIFF!...AND I DIDN'T SEE HIM AGAIN! SNIFF!...
A BEAVER AND TWO RACCOONS HAVE DISAPPEARED...
...WE'RE SEARCHING FOR THEM...
I HAVE THE FEELING THAT SOMETHING BAD HAS HAPPENED TO HIM TOO. WHAT SHOULD WE DO?

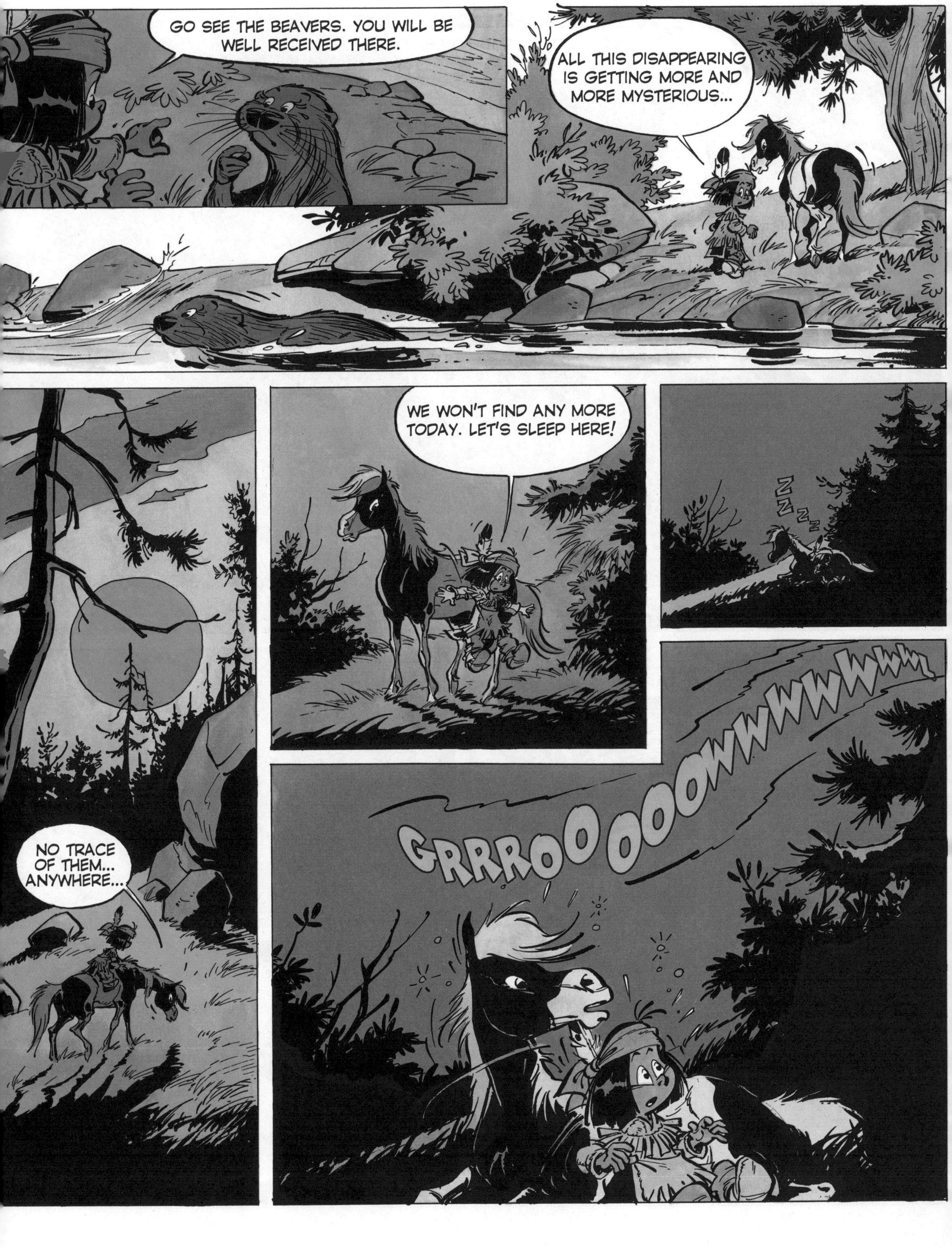
GO SEE THE BEAVERS. YOU WILL BE WELL RECEIVED THERE.
ALL THIS DISAPPEARING IS GETTING MORE AND MORE MYSTERIOUS...
NO TRACE OF THEM... ANYWHERE...
WE WON'T FIND ANY MORE TODAY. LET'S SLEEP HERE!
Z Z Z
GRRROOOOOOWWWWWWWL

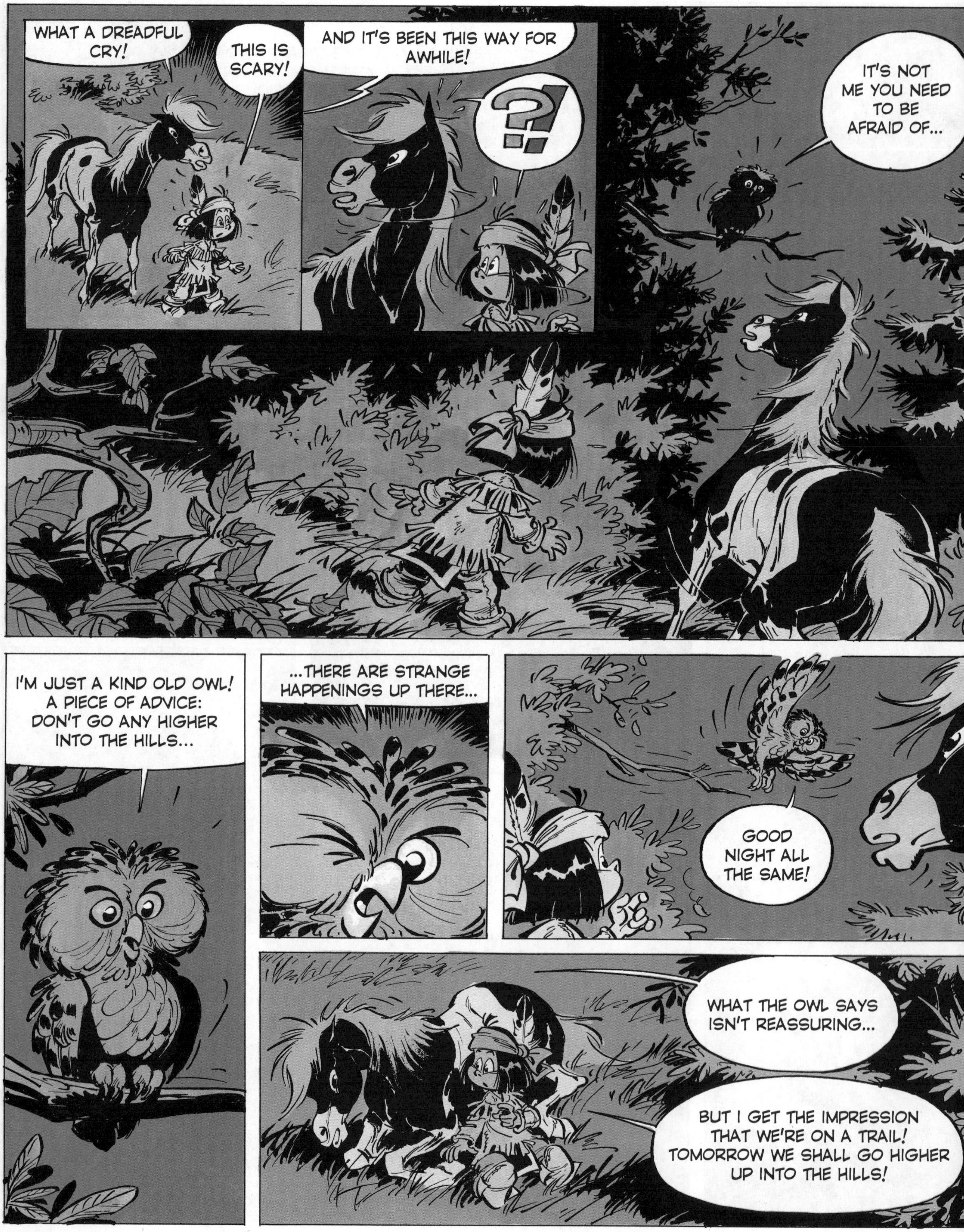
WHAT A DREADFUL CRY!
THIS IS SCARY!
AND IT'S BEEN THIS WAY FOR AWHILE!
?!
IT'S NOT ME YOU NEED TO BE AFRAID OF...
I'M JUST A KIND OLD OWL! A PIECE OF ADVICE: DON'T GO ANY HIGHER INTO THE HILLS...
...THERE ARE STRANGE HAPPENINGS UP THERE...
GOOD NIGHT ALL THE SAME!
WHAT THE OWL SAYS ISN'T REASSURING...
BUT I GET THE IMPRESSION THAT WE'RE ON A TRAIL! TOMORROW WE SHALL GO HIGHER UP INTO THE HILLS!

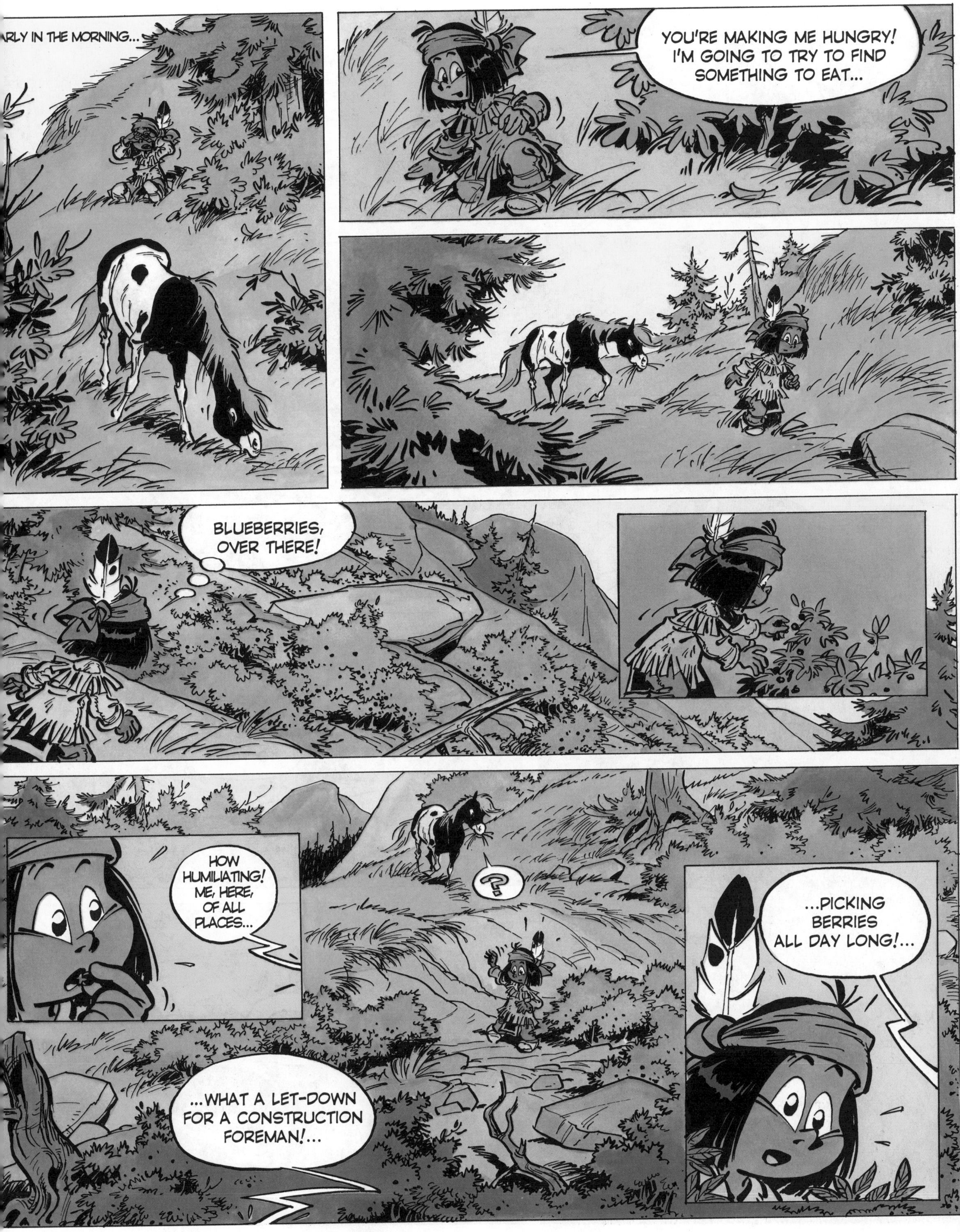

ARLY IN THE MORNING...
YOU'RE MAKING ME HUNGRY! I'M GOING TO TRY TO FIND SOMETHING TO EAT...
BLUEBERRIES, OVER THERE!
HOW HUMILIATING! ME, HERE, OF ALL PLACES...
...WHAT A LET-DOWN FOR A CONSTRUCTION FOREMAN!...
?
...PICKING BERRIES ALL DAY LONG!...

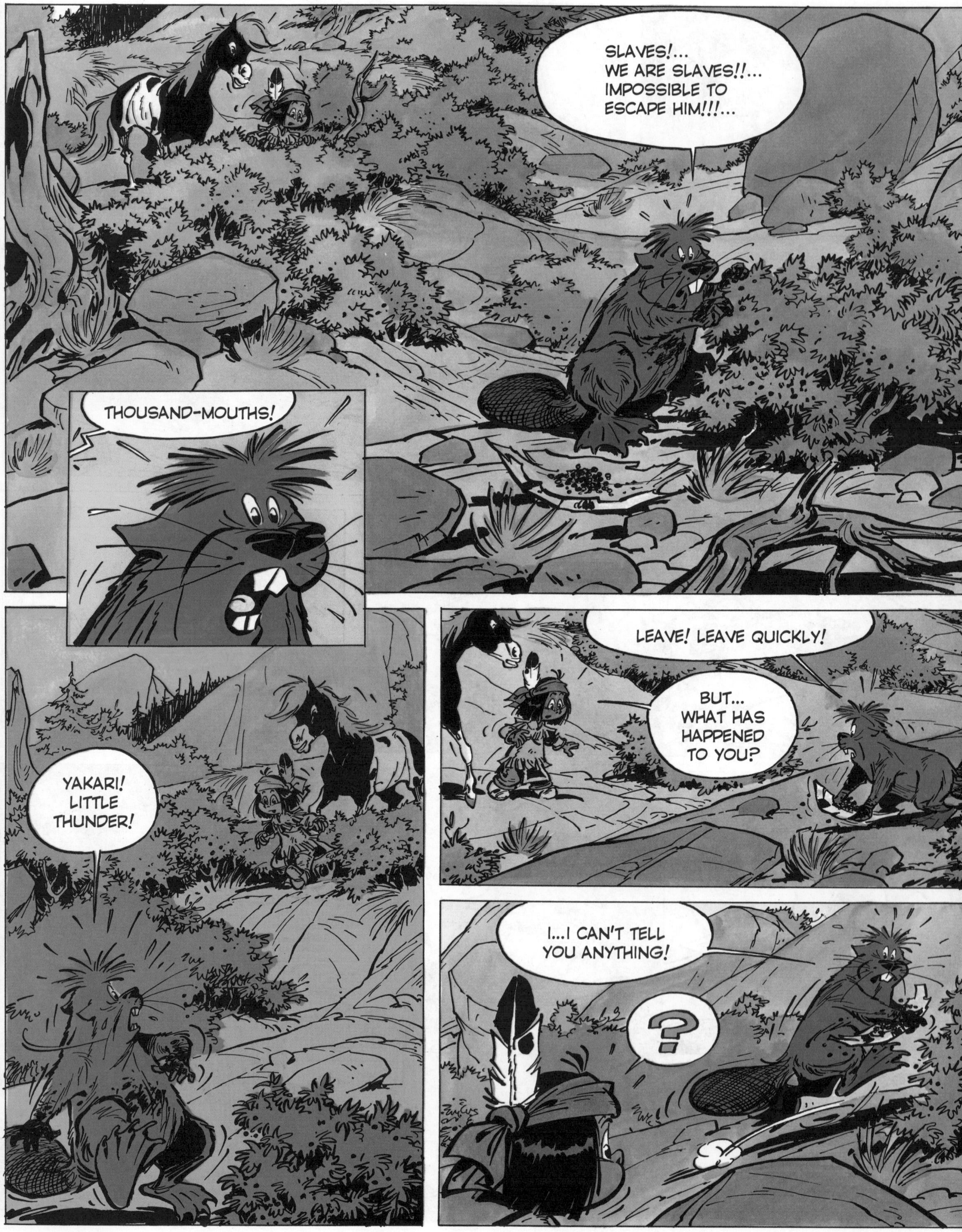
SLAVES!...
WE ARE SLAVES!!...
IMPOSSIBLE TO
ESCAPE HIM!!!...
THOUSAND-MOUTHS!
YAKARI!
LITTLE
THUNDER!
LEAVE! LEAVE QUICKLY!
BUT...
WHAT HAS
HAPPENED
TO YOU?
I...I CAN'T TELL
YOU ANYTHING!
?

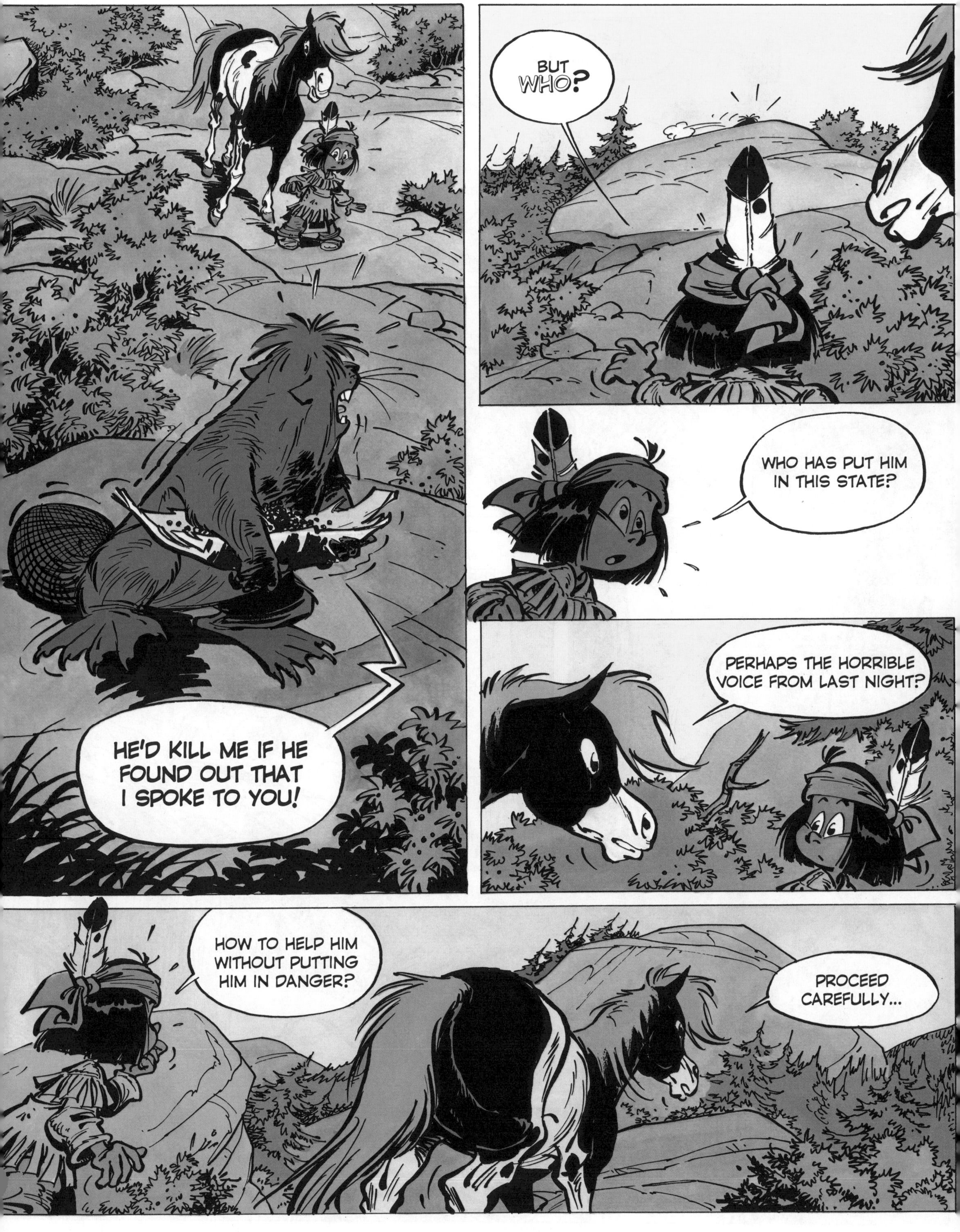
HE'D KILL ME IF HE FOUND OUT THAT I SPOKE TO YOU!
BUT WHO?
WHO HAS PUT HIM IN THIS STATE?
PERHAPS THE HORRIBLE VOICE FROM LAST NIGHT?
HOW TO HELP HIM WITHOUT PUTTING HIM IN DANGER?
PROCEED CAREFULLY...

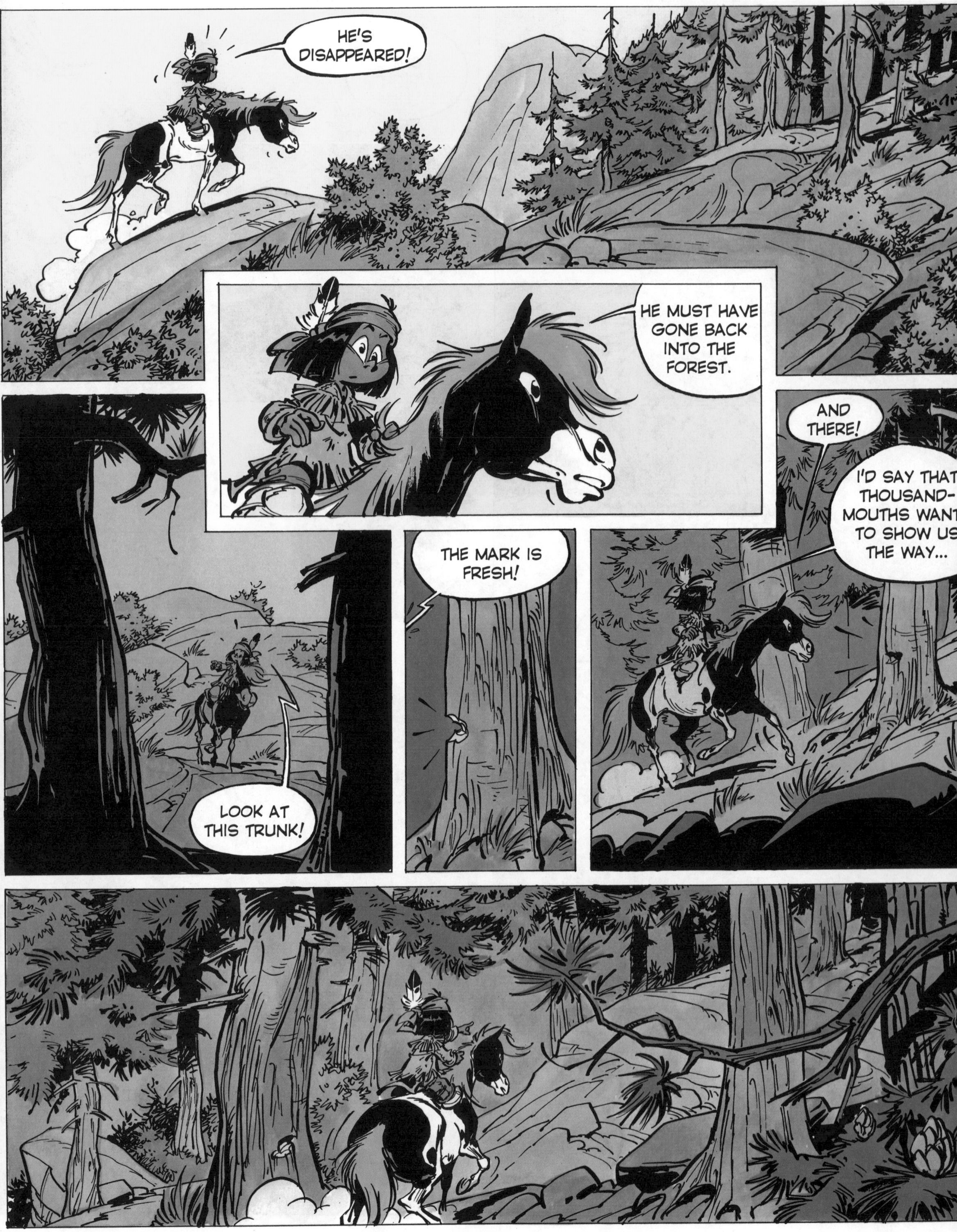
HE'S DISAPPEARED!
HE MUST HAVE GONE BACK INTO THE FOREST.
LOOK AT THIS TRUNK!
THE MARK IS FRESH!
AND THERE!
I'D SAY THAT THOUSAND-MOUTHS WANT TO SHOW US THE WAY...

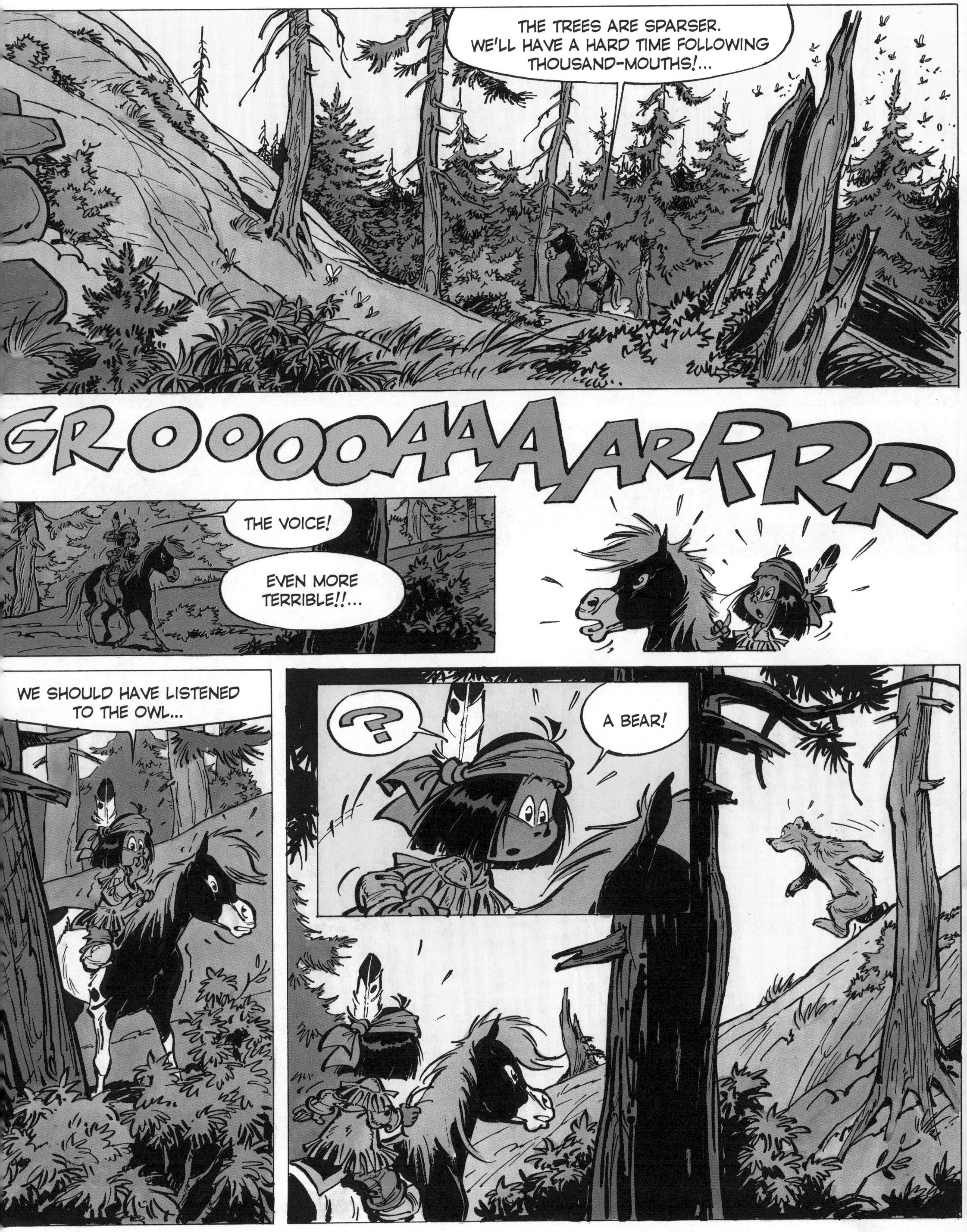

THE TREES ARE SPARSER. WE'LL HAVE A HARD TIME FOLLOWING THOUSAND-MOUTHS!...
GROOOOAAAARRRR
THE VOICE!
EVEN MORE TERRIBLE!!...
WE SHOULD HAVE LISTENED TO THE OWL...
?
A BEAR!

THAT WAS HIS, THAT VOICE!...

BUT...HE'S HARVESTING SOME HONEY...

DO YOU THINK HE'S THE ONE TERRORIZING THOUSAND-MOUTHS? HE DOESN'T REALLY SEEM VICIOUS, THOUGH...

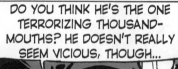

I AM GOING TO TRY TO TALK TO HIM...

HEY! BEAR!

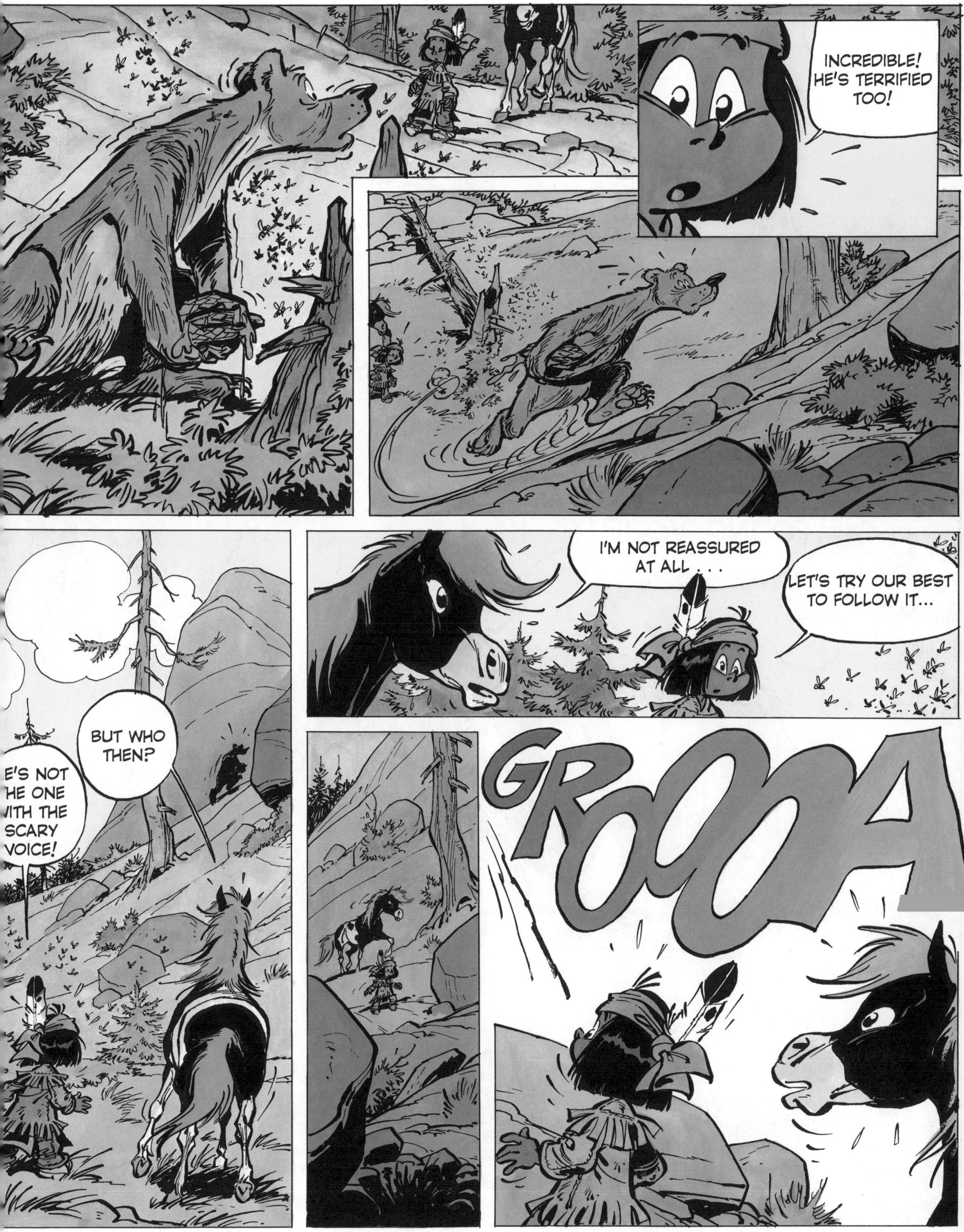
INCREDIBLE! HE'S TERRIFIED TOO!
I'M NOT REASSURED AT ALL . . .
LET'S TRY OUR BEST TO FOLLOW IT...
E'S NOT HE ONE WITH THE SCARY VOICE!
BUT WHO THEN?
GROOOA

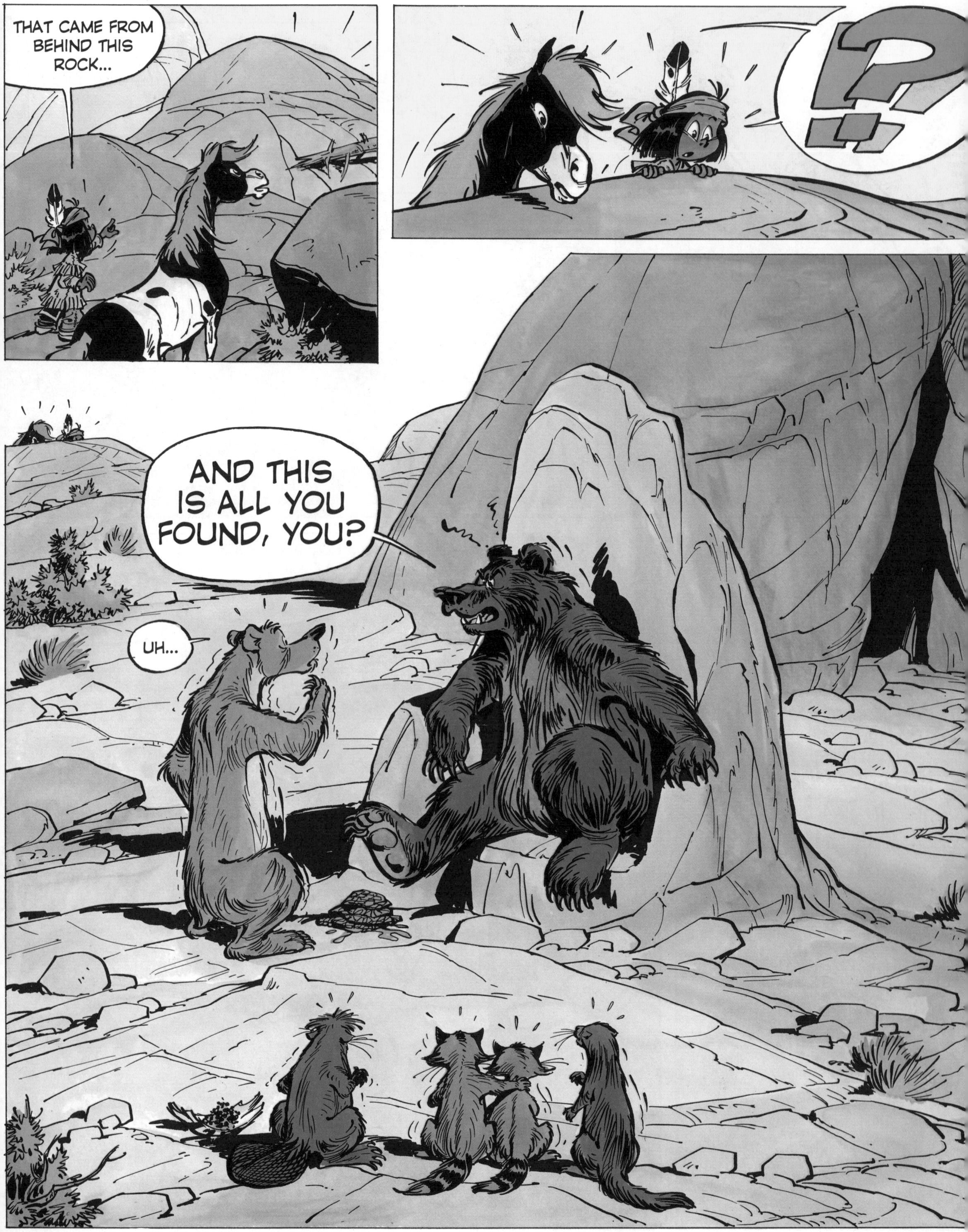
THAT CAME FROM BEHIND THIS ROCK...
AND THIS IS ALL YOU FOUND, YOU?
UH...

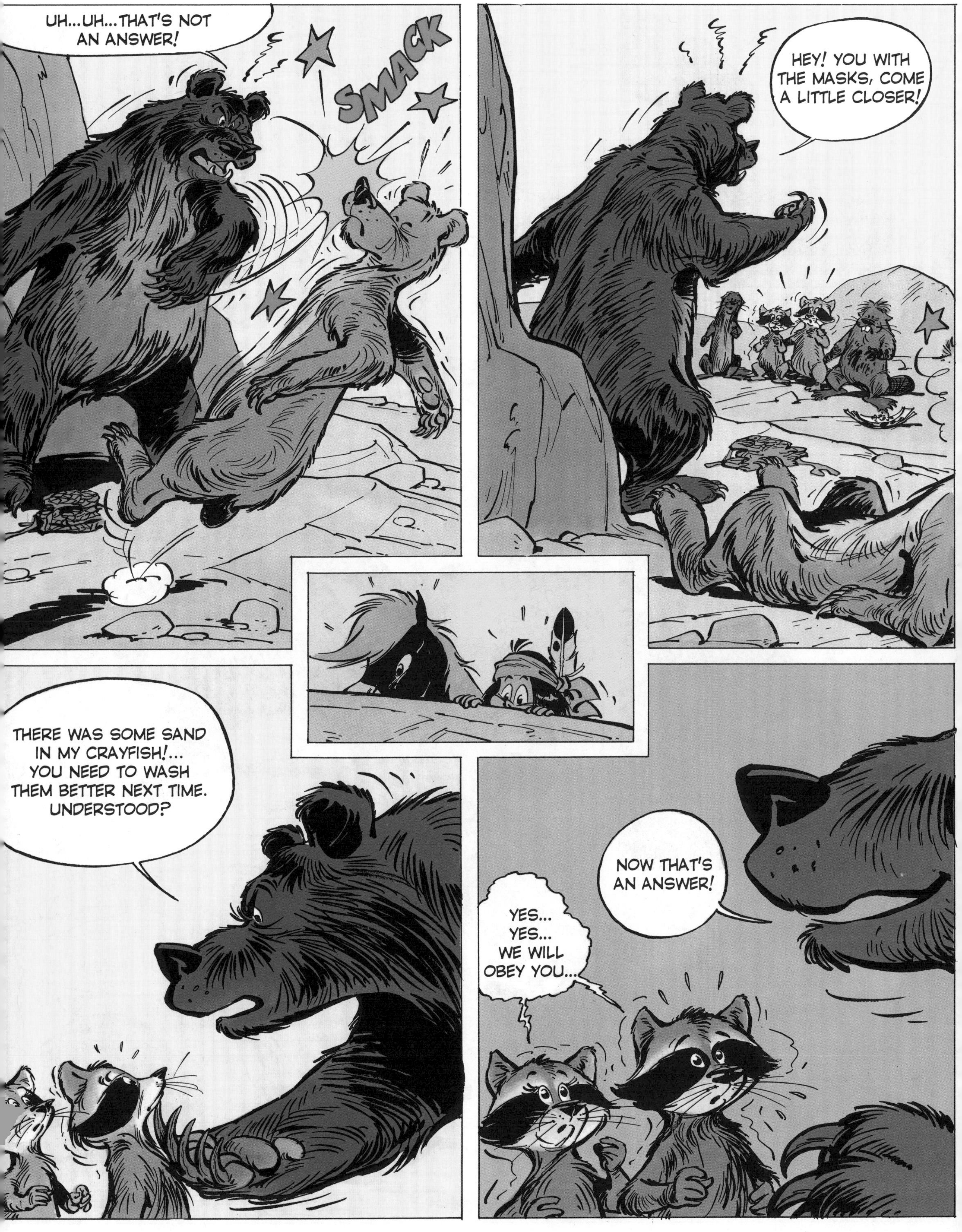

UH...UH...THAT'S NOT AN ANSWER!
SMACK
HEY! YOU WITH THE MASKS, COME A LITTLE CLOSER!
THERE WAS SOME SAND IN MY CRAYFISH!... YOU NEED TO WASH THEM BETTER NEXT TIME. UNDERSTOOD?
YES... YES... WE WILL OBEY YOU...
NOW THAT'S AN ANSWER!

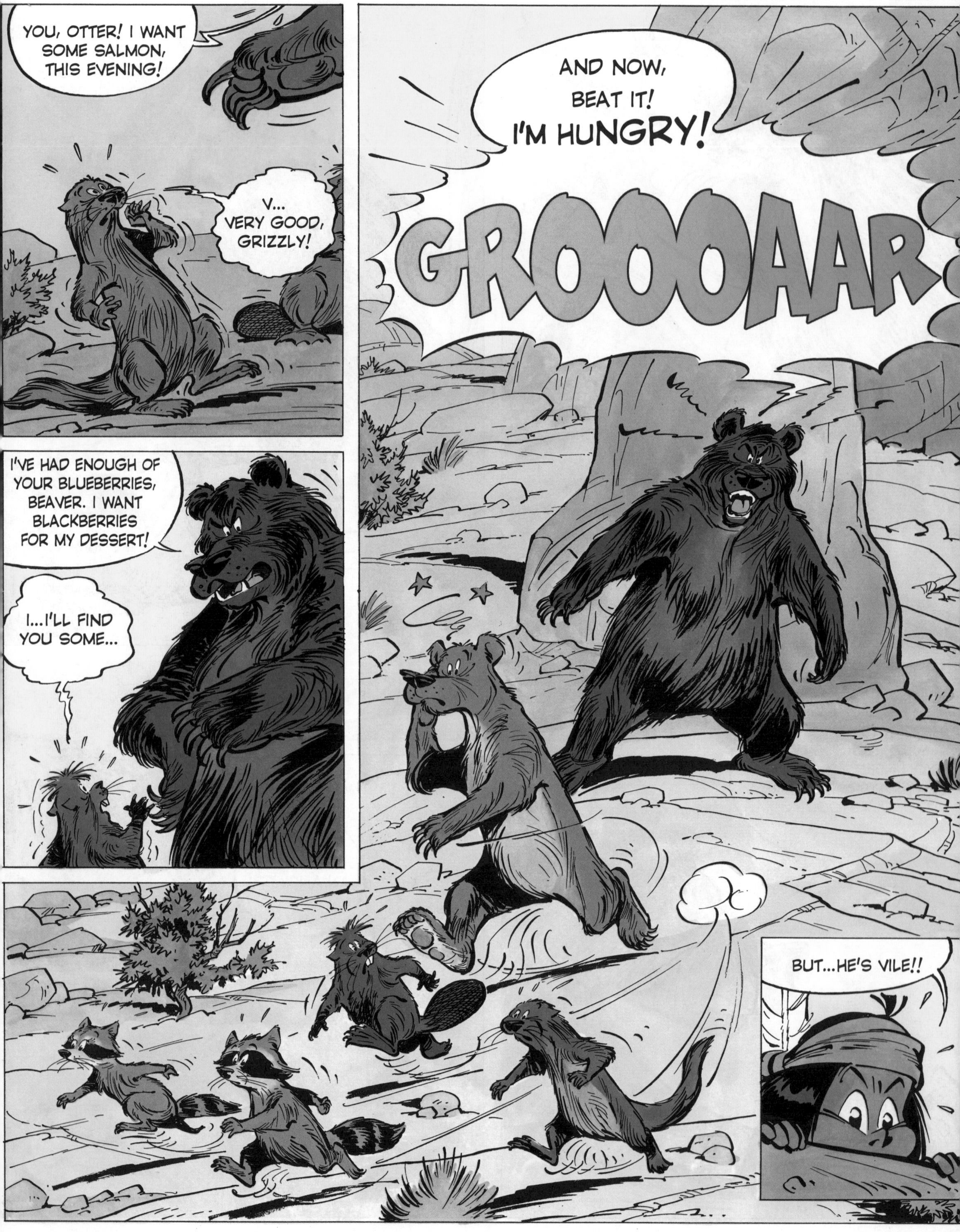
YOU, OTTER! I WANT SOME SALMON, THIS EVENING!
V... VERY GOOD, GRIZZLY!
I'VE HAD ENOUGH OF YOUR BLUEBERRIES, BEAVER. I WANT BLACKBERRIES FOR MY DESSERT!
I...I'LL FIND YOU SOME...
AND NOW, BEAT IT! I'M HUNGRY!
GROOOAAR
BUT...HE'S VILE!!

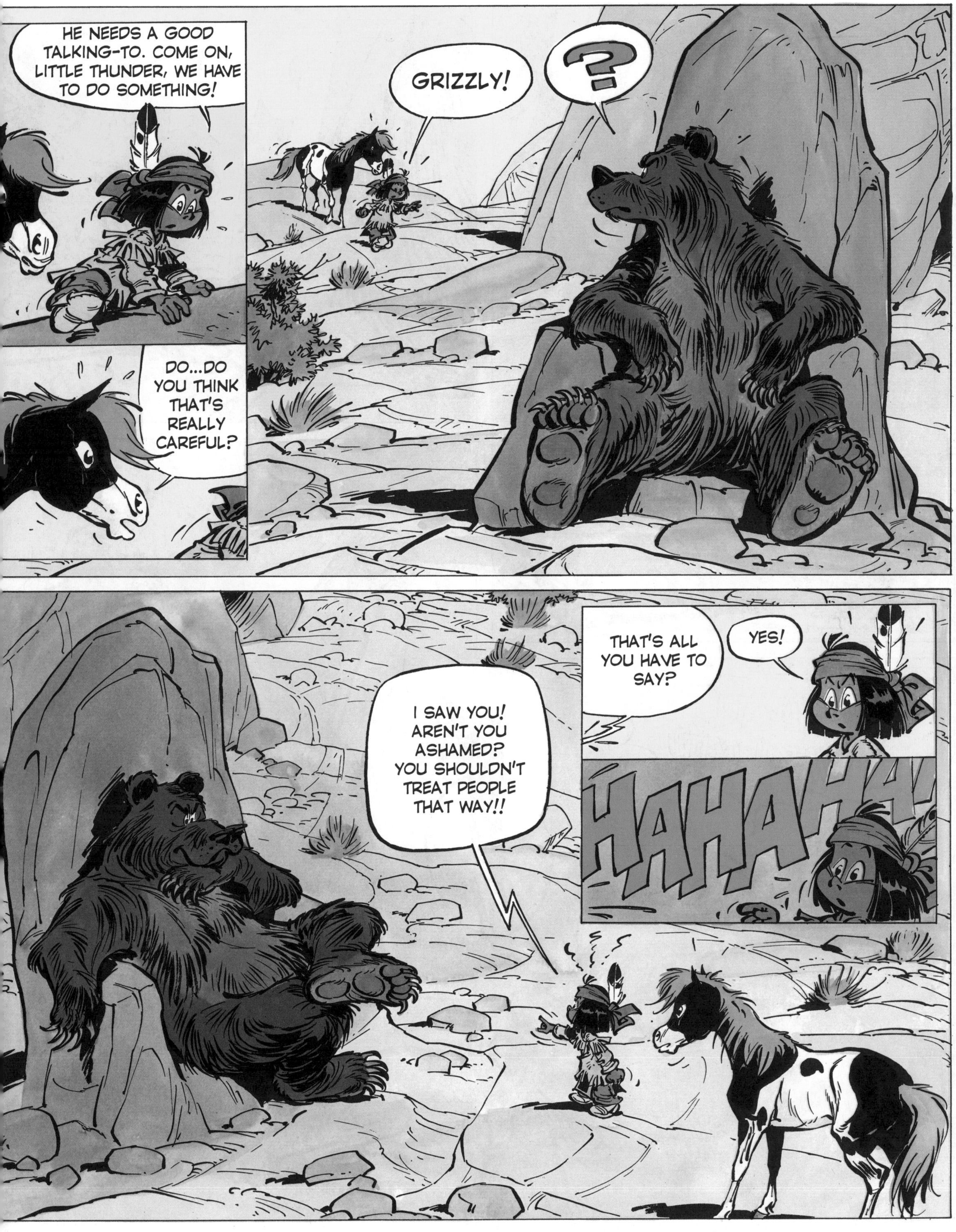
HE NEEDS A GOOD TALKING-TO. COME ON, LITTLE THUNDER, WE HAVE TO DO SOMETHING!
GRIZZLY!
?
DO...DO YOU THINK THAT'S REALLY CAREFUL?
I SAW YOU! AREN'T YOU ASHAMED? YOU SHOULDN'T TREAT PEOPLE THAT WAY!!
THAT'S ALL YOU HAVE TO SAY?
YES!
HAHAHA!

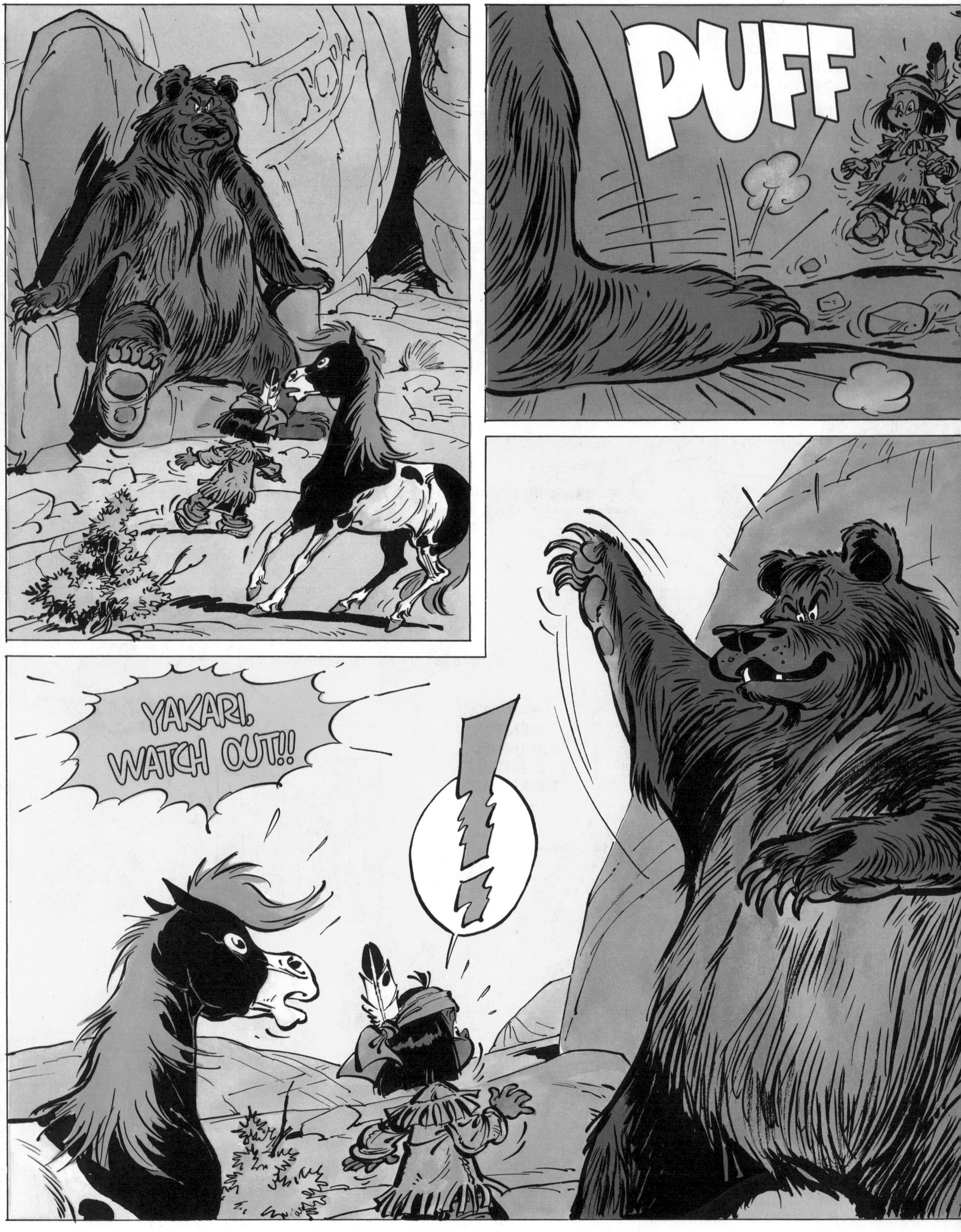
PUFF
YAKARI, WATCH OUT!!
!

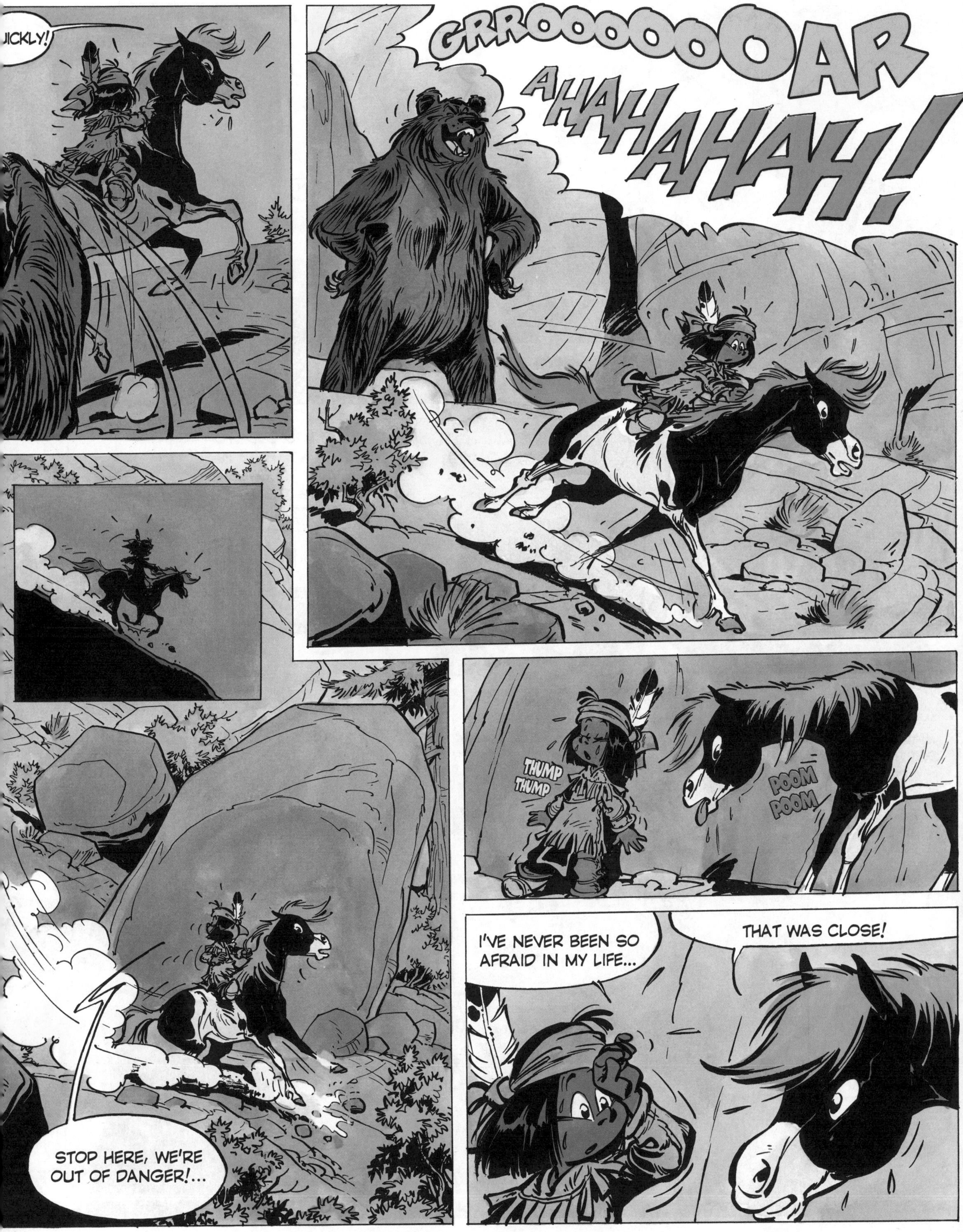

UICKLY!
GRROOOOOOOOAR
AHAHAHAHAH!
THUMP THUMP
POOM POOM
STOP HERE, WE'RE OUT OF DANGER!...
I'VE NEVER BEEN SO AFRAID IN MY LIFE...
THAT WAS CLOSE!

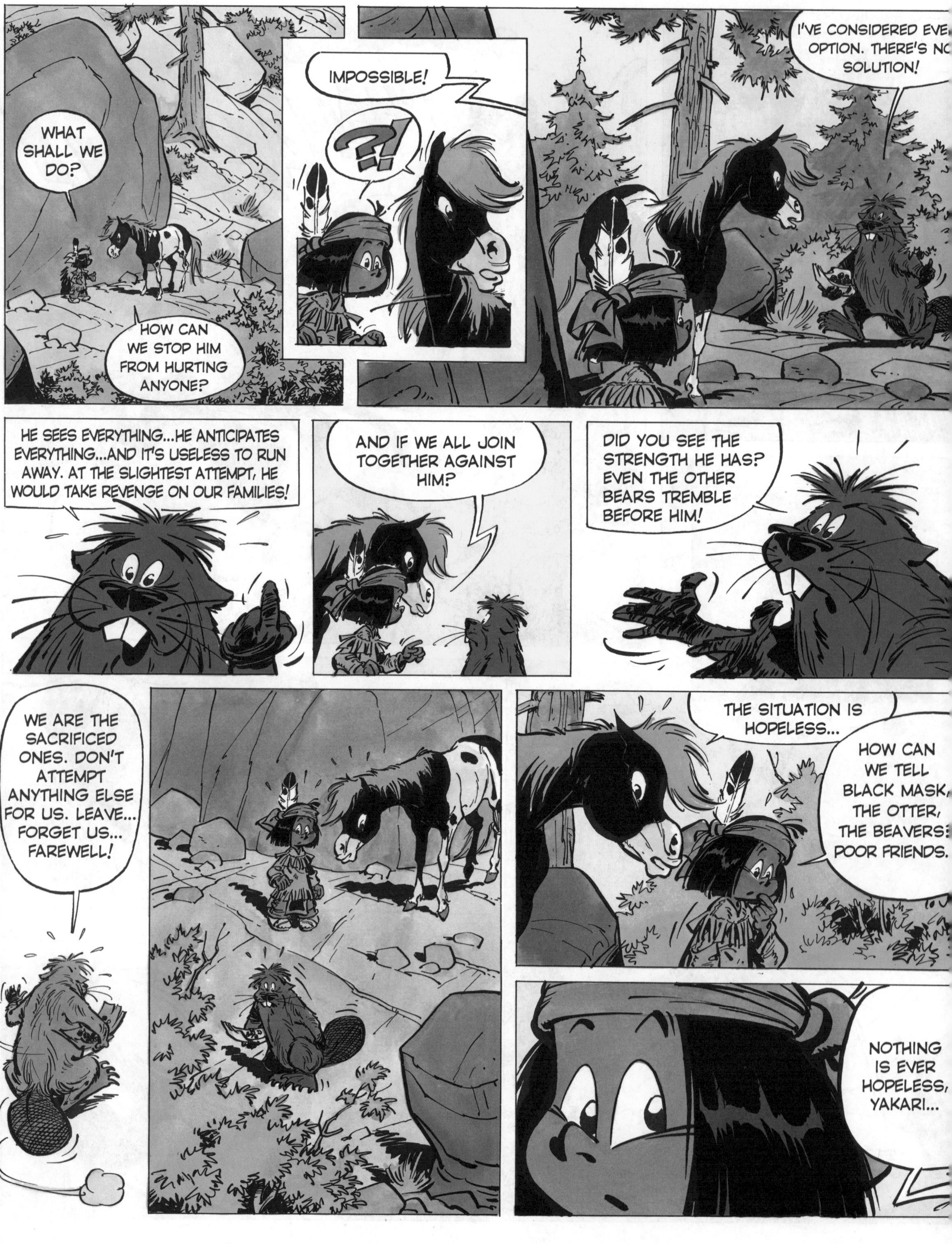

WHAT SHALL WE DO?
HOW CAN WE STOP HIM FROM HURTING ANYONE?
IMPOSSIBLE!
?!
I'VE CONSIDERED EVE
OPTION. THERE'S NO
SOLUTION!
HE SEES EVERYTHING...HE ANTICIPATES EVERYTHING...AND IT'S USELESS TO RUN AWAY. AT THE SLIGHTEST ATTEMPT, HE WOULD TAKE REVENGE ON OUR FAMILIES!
AND IF WE ALL JOIN TOGETHER AGAINST HIM?
DID YOU SEE THE STRENGTH HE HAS? EVEN THE OTHER BEARS TREMBLE BEFORE HIM!
WE ARE THE SACRIFICED ONES. DON'T ATTEMPT ANYTHING ELSE FOR US. LEAVE... FORGET US... FAREWELL!
THE SITUATION IS HOPELESS...
HOW CAN WE TELL BLACK MASK, THE OTTER, THE BEAVERS: POOR FRIENDS.
NOTHING IS EVER HOPELESS, YAKARI...

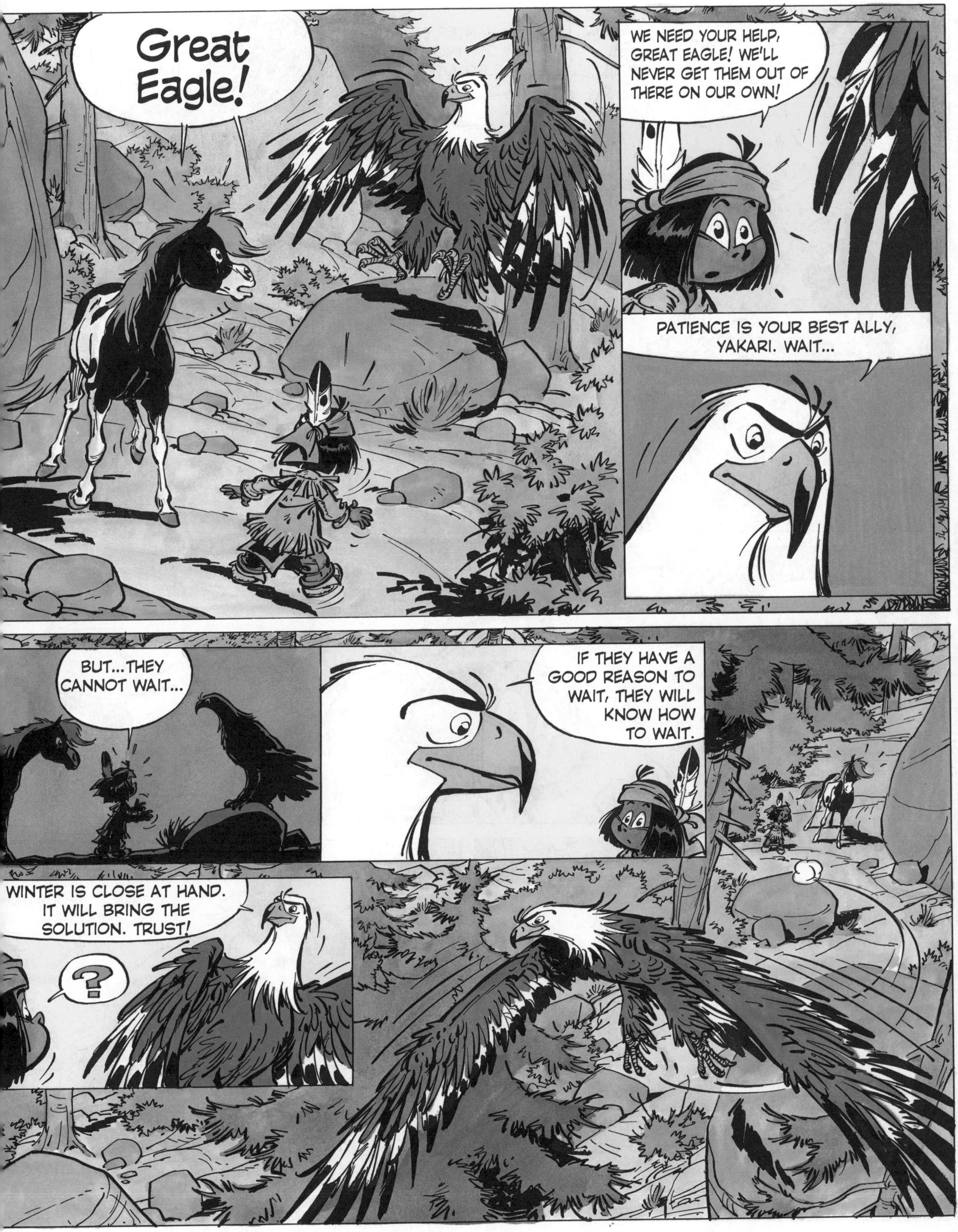
Great Eagle!
WE NEED YOUR HELP, GREAT EAGLE! WE'LL NEVER GET THEM OUT OF THERE ON OUR OWN!
PATIENCE IS YOUR BEST ALLY, YAKARI. WAIT...
BUT...THEY CANNOT WAIT...
IF THEY HAVE A GOOD REASON TO WAIT, THEY WILL KNOW HOW TO WAIT.
WINTER IS CLOSE AT HAND. IT WILL BRING THE SOLUTION. TRUST!
?

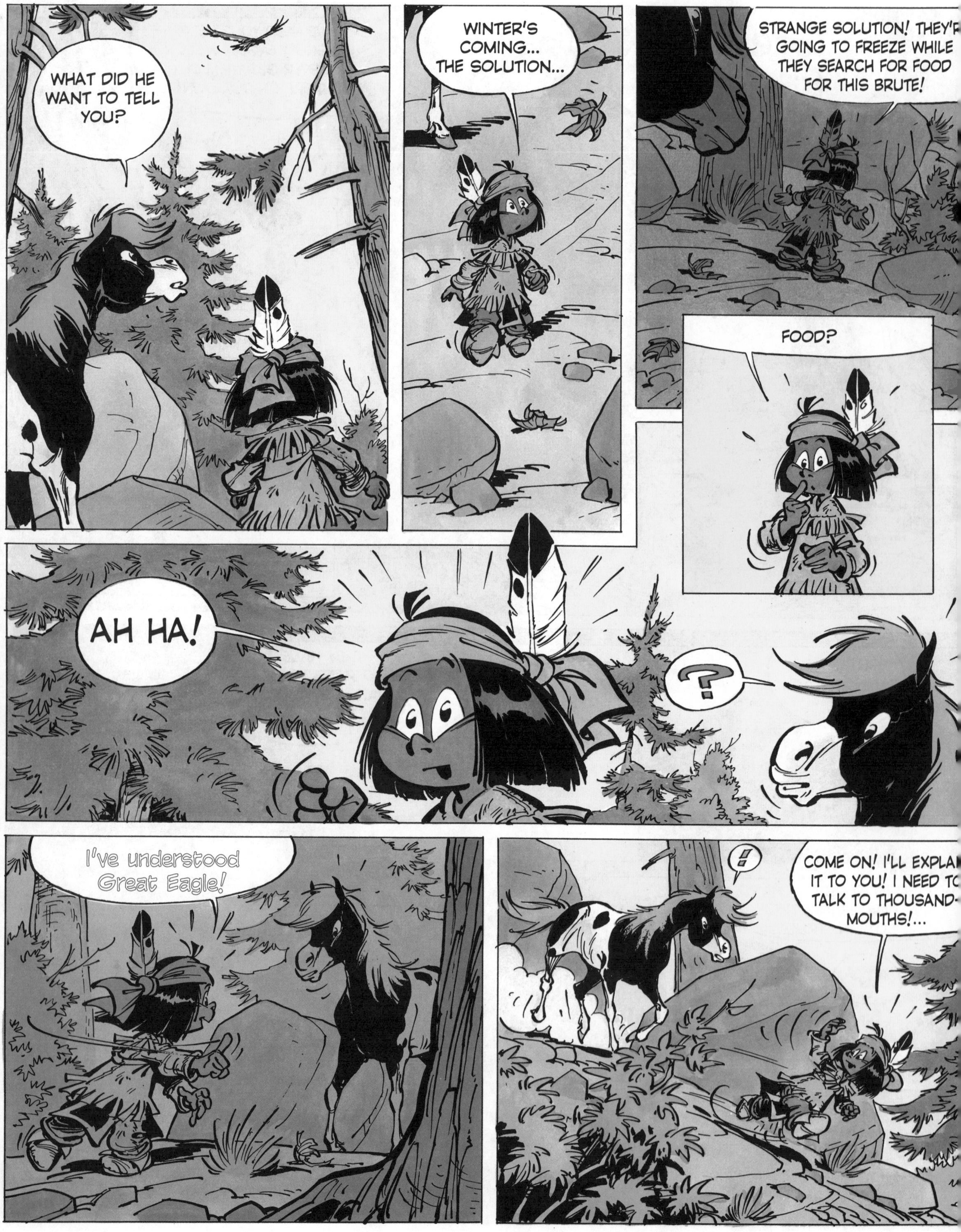
WHAT DID HE WANT TO TELL YOU?
WINTER'S COMING... THE SOLUTION...
STRANGE SOLUTION! THEY'R GOING TO FREEZE WHILE THEY SEARCH FOR FOOD FOR THIS BRUTE!
FOOD?
AH HA!
?
I've understood Great Eagle!
!
COME ON! I'LL EXPLA IT TO YOU! I NEED TO TALK TO THOUSAND-MOUTHS!...

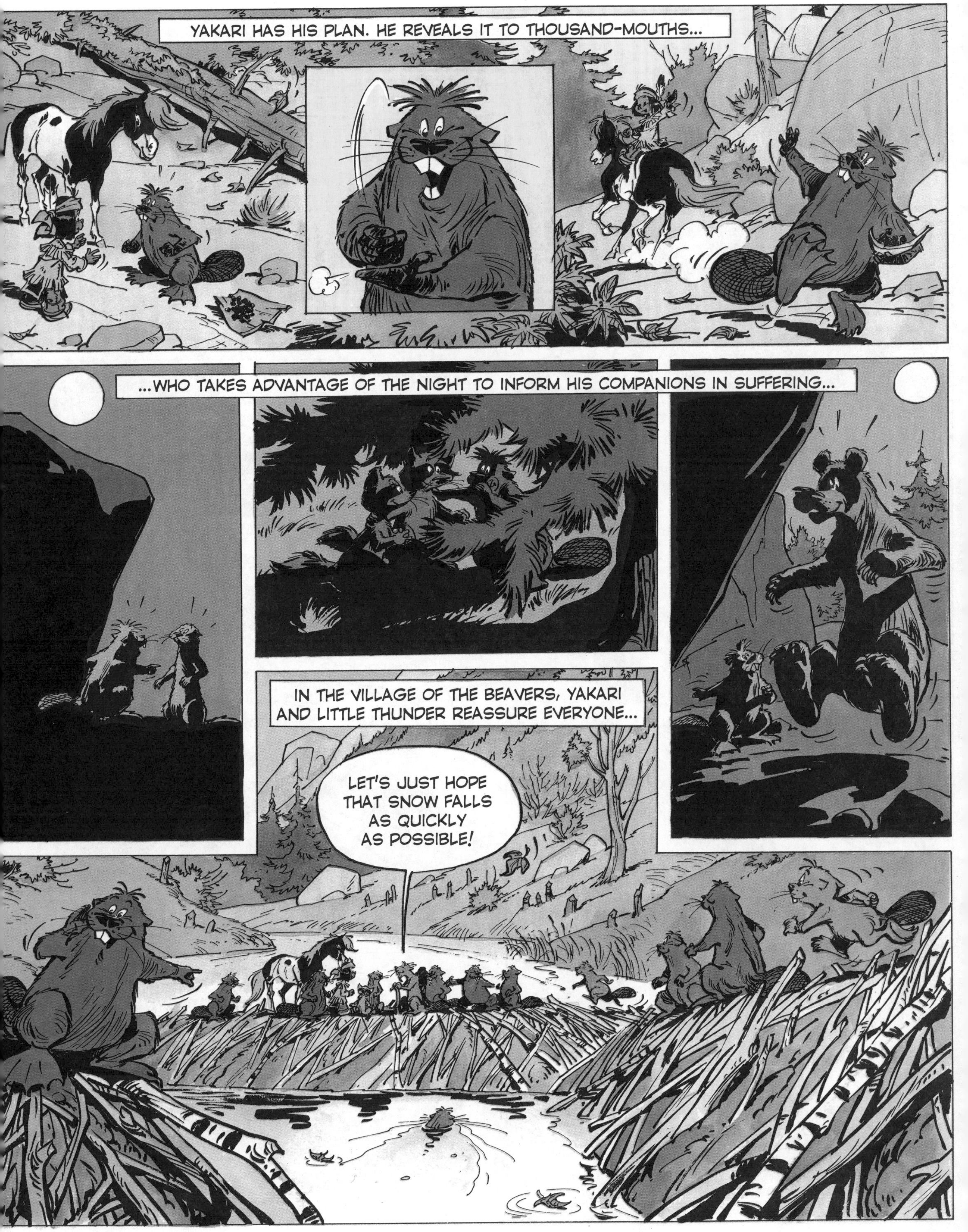
YAKARI HAS HIS PLAN. HE REVEALS IT TO THOUSAND-MOUTHS...
...WHO TAKES ADVANTAGE OF THE NIGHT TO INFORM HIS COMPANIONS IN SUFFERING...
IN THE VILLAGE OF THE BEAVERS, YAKARI AND LITTLE THUNDER REASSURE EVERYONE...
LET'S JUST HOPE THAT SNOW FALLS AS QUICKLY AS POSSIBLE!

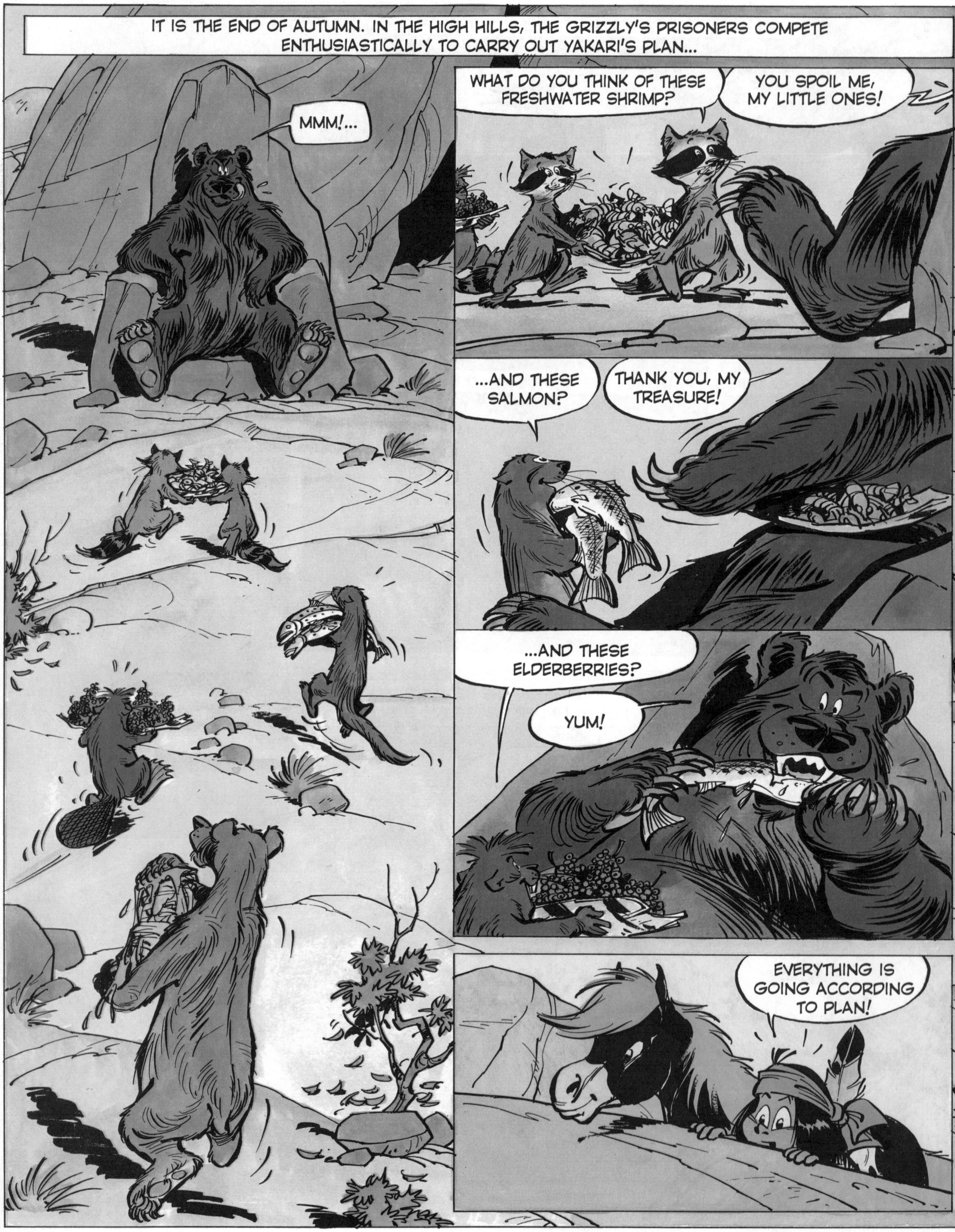
IT IS THE END OF AUTUMN. IN THE HIGH HILLS, THE GRIZZLY'S PRISONERS COMPETE ENTHUSIASTICALLY TO CARRY OUT YAKARI'S PLAN...
MMM!...
WHAT DO YOU THINK OF THESE FRESHWATER SHRIMP?
YOU SPOIL ME, MY LITTLE ONES!
...AND THESE SALMON?
THANK YOU, MY TREASURE!
...AND THESE ELDERBERRIES?
YUM!
EVERYTHING IS GOING ACCORDING TO PLAN!

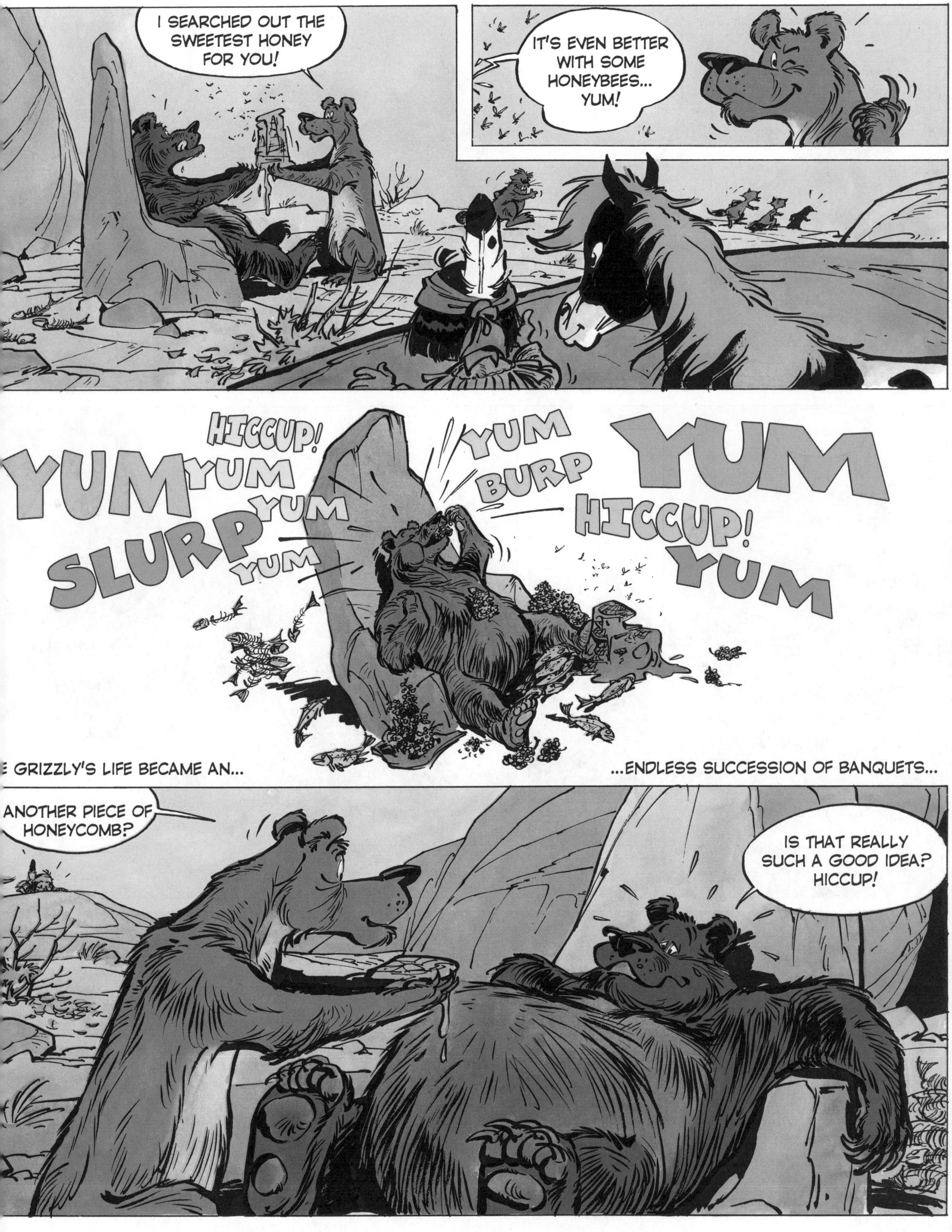
I SEARCHED OUT THE SWEETEST HONEY FOR YOU!
IT'S EVEN BETTER WITH SOME HONEYBEES... YUM!
HICCUP!
YUM
YUM
YUM
SLURP
YUM
YUM
BURP
YUM
HICCUP!
YUM
E GRIZZLY'S LIFE BECAME AN...
...ENDLESS SUCCESSION OF BANQUETS...
ANOTHER PIECE OF HONEYCOMB?
IS THAT REALLY SUCH A GOOD IDEA? HICCUP!

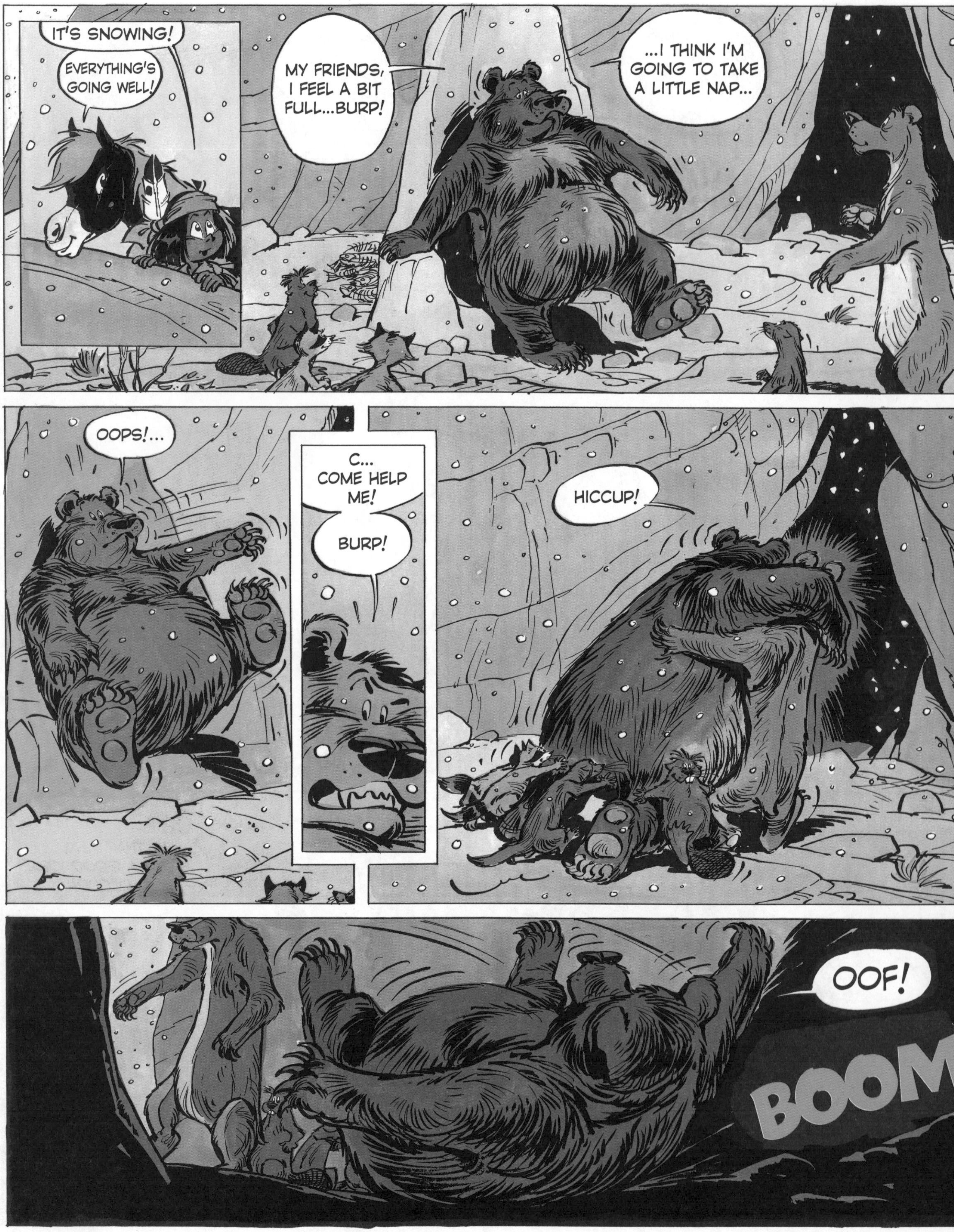
IT'S SNOWING!
EVERYTHING'S GOING WELL!
MY FRIENDS, I FEEL A BIT FULL...BURP!
...I THINK I'M GOING TO TAKE A LITTLE NAP...
OOPS!...
C... COME HELP ME!
BURP!
HICCUP!
OOF!
BOOM

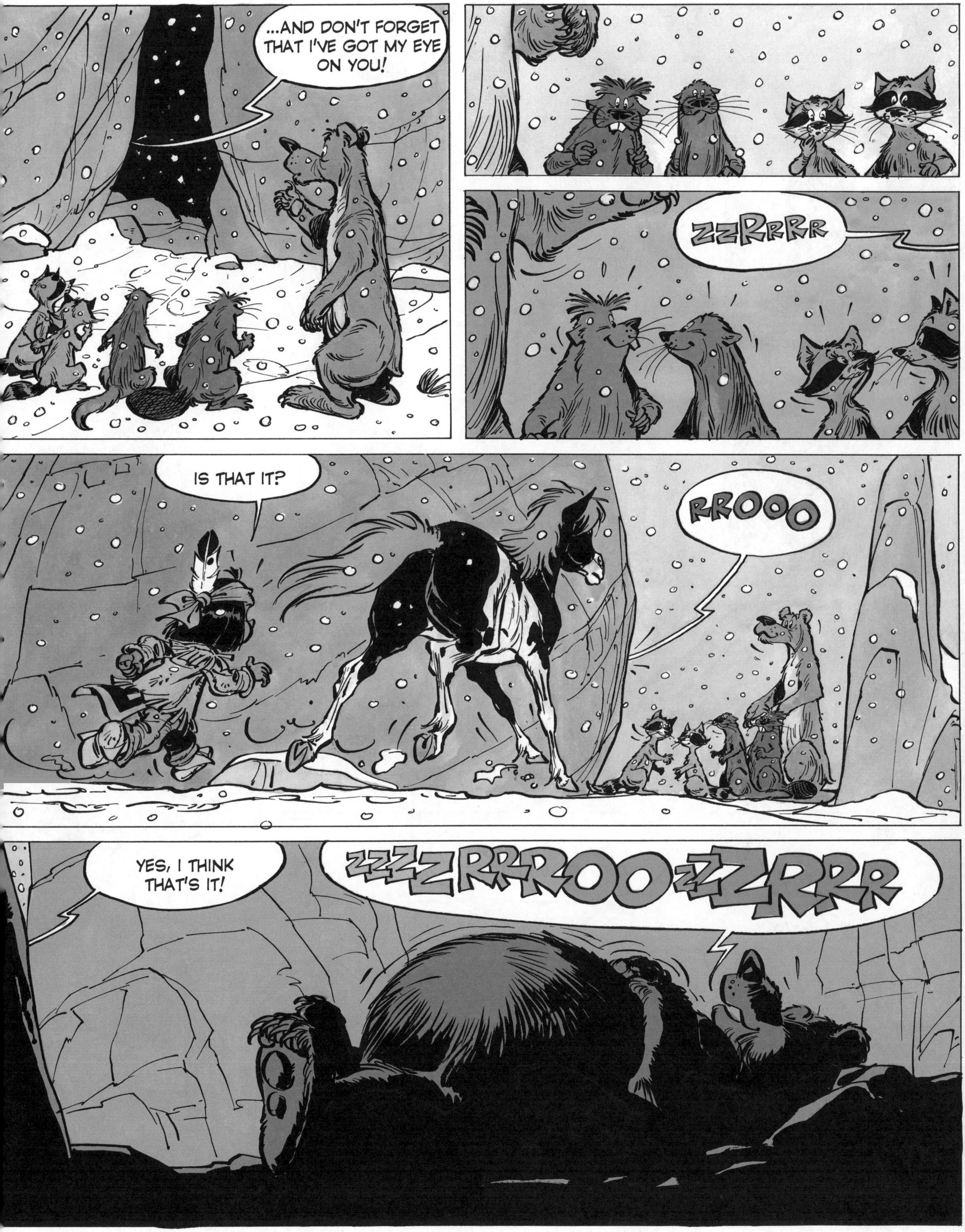
...AND DON'T FORGET THAT I'VE GOT MY EYE ON YOU!
ZZRRRR
IS THAT IT?
RROOO
YES, I THINK THAT'S IT!
ZZZZRRRROOZZZRRRR

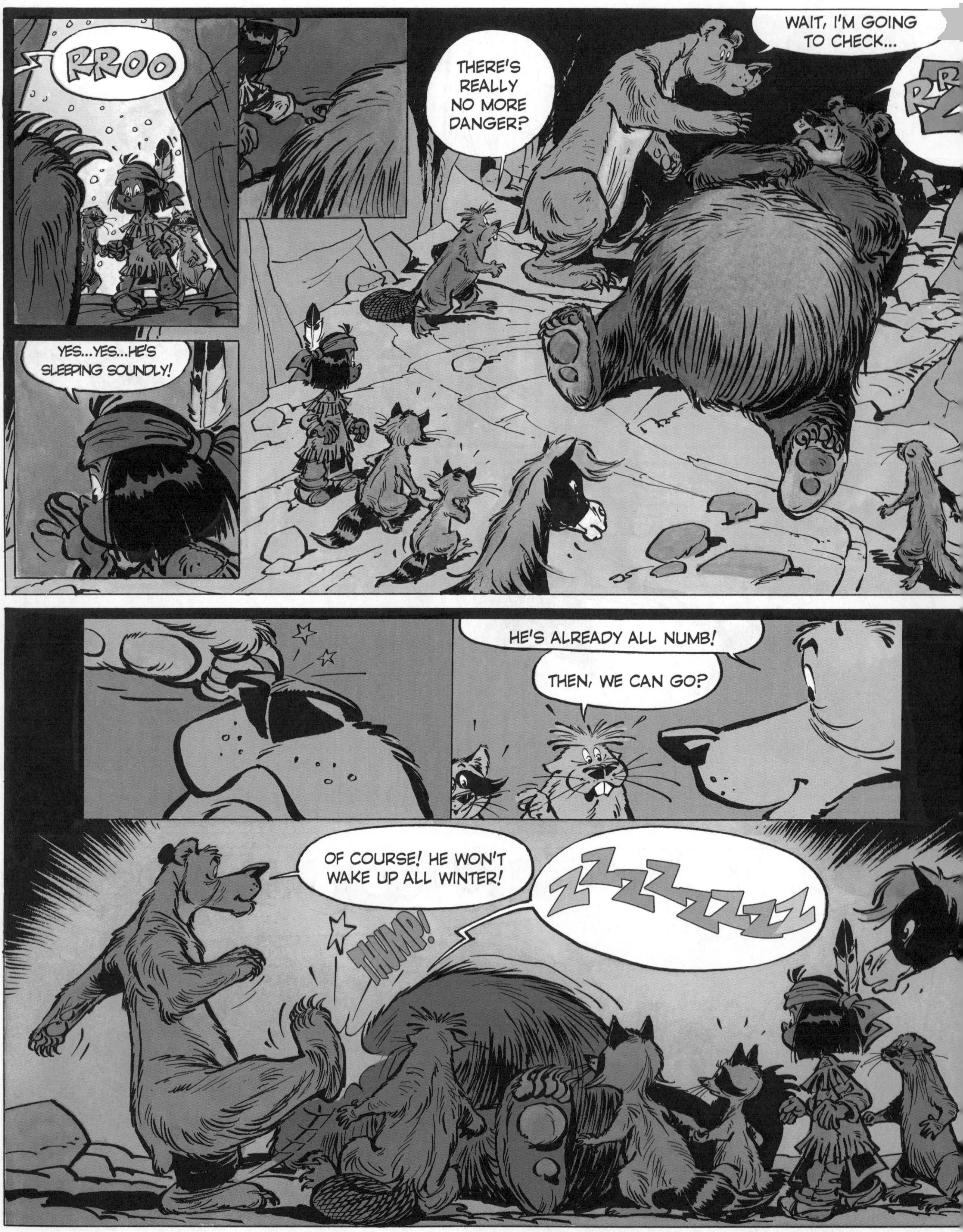
RROO
THERE'S REALLY NO MORE DANGER?
WAIT, I'M GOING TO CHECK...
YES...YES...HE'S SLEEPING SOUNDLY!
HE'S ALREADY ALL NUMB!
THEN, WE CAN GO?
OF COURSE! HE WON'T WAKE UP ALL WINTER!
THUMP!
ZZZZZZZZZ

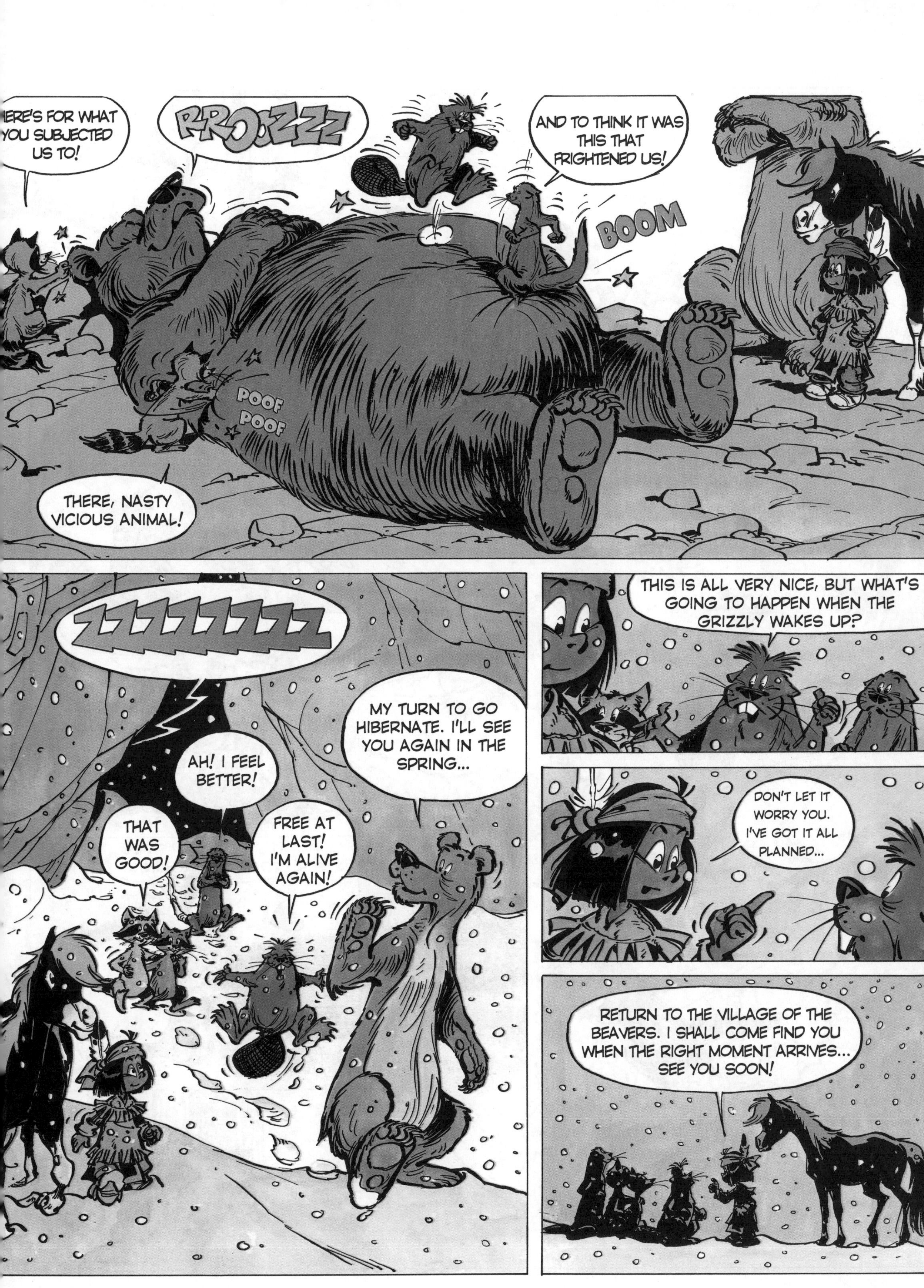
ERE'S FOR WHAT YOU SUBJECTED US TO!
RROZZZ
AND TO THINK IT WAS THIS THAT FRIGHTENED US!
BOOM
POOF POOF
THERE, NASTY VICIOUS ANIMAL!
ZZZZZZZZZ
AH! I FEEL BETTER!
THAT WAS GOOD!
FREE AT LAST! I'M ALIVE AGAIN!
MY TURN TO GO HIBERNATE. I'LL SEE YOU AGAIN IN THE SPRING...
THIS IS ALL VERY NICE, BUT WHAT'S GOING TO HAPPEN WHEN THE GRIZZLY WAKES UP?
DON'T LET IT WORRY YOU. I'VE GOT IT ALL PLANNED...
RETURN TO THE VILLAGE OF THE BEAVERS. I SHALL COME FIND YOU WHEN THE RIGHT MOMENT ARRIVES... SEE YOU SOON!

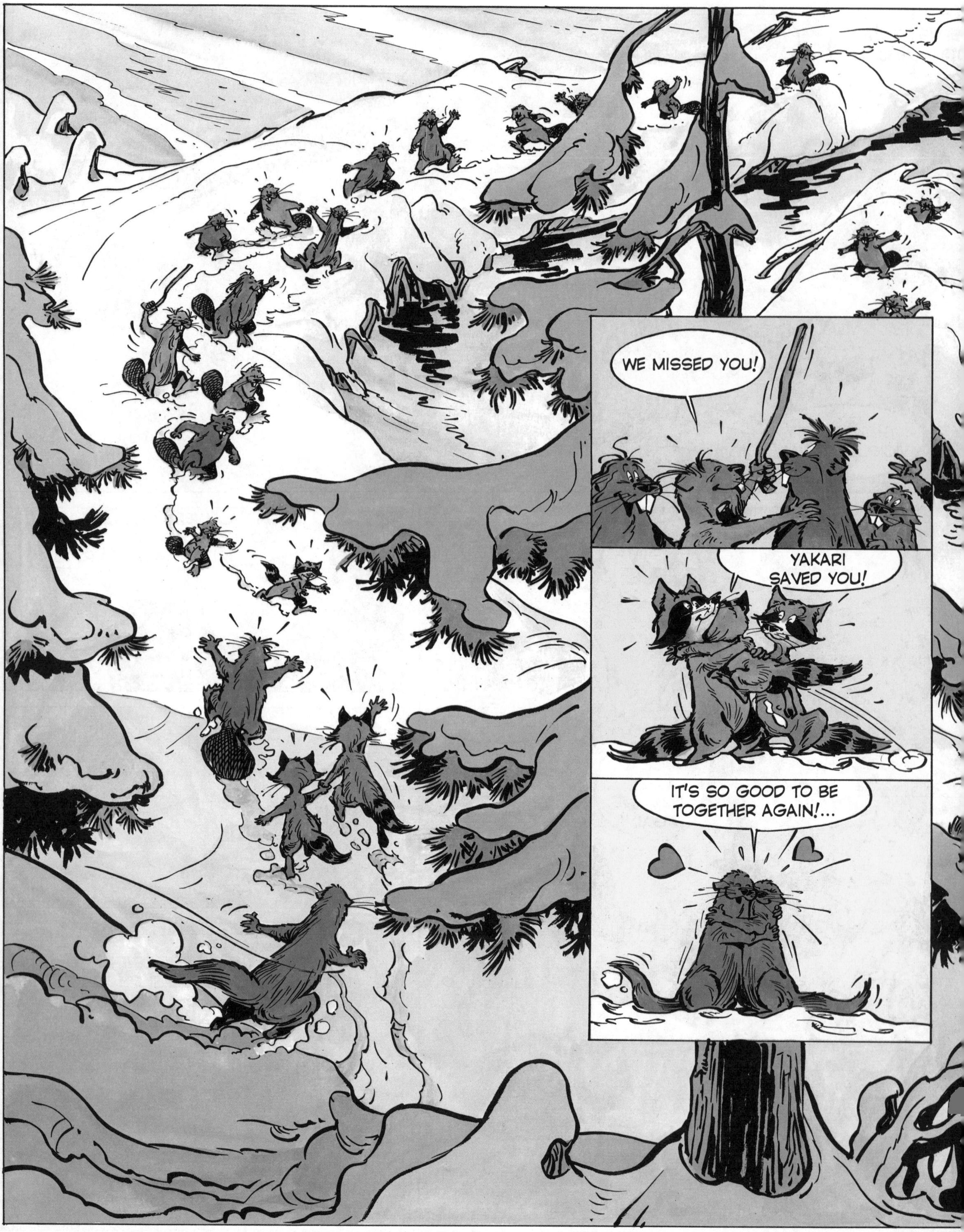
WE MISSED YOU!
YAKARI SAVED YOU!
IT'S SO GOOD TO BE TOGETHER AGAIN!...

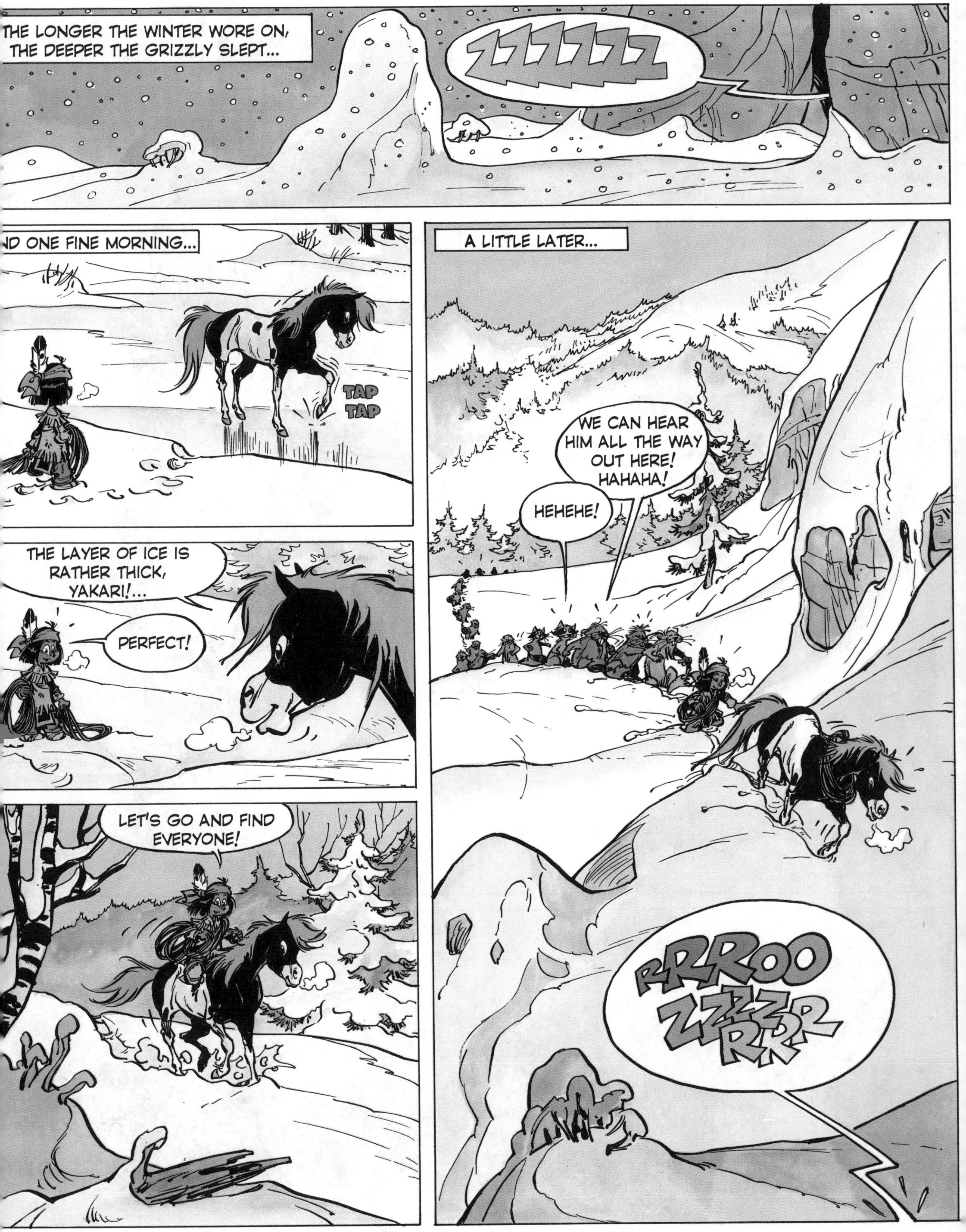

THE LONGER THE WINTER WORE ON, THE DEEPER THE GRIZZLY SLEPT...
ZZZZZZZ
ND ONE FINE MORNING...
TAP TAP
THE LAYER OF ICE IS RATHER THICK, YAKARI!...
PERFECT!
LET'S GO AND FIND EVERYONE!
A LITTLE LATER...
WE CAN HEAR HIM ALL THE WAY OUT HERE! HAHAHA!
HEHEHE!
RRROO ZZZZR RRR

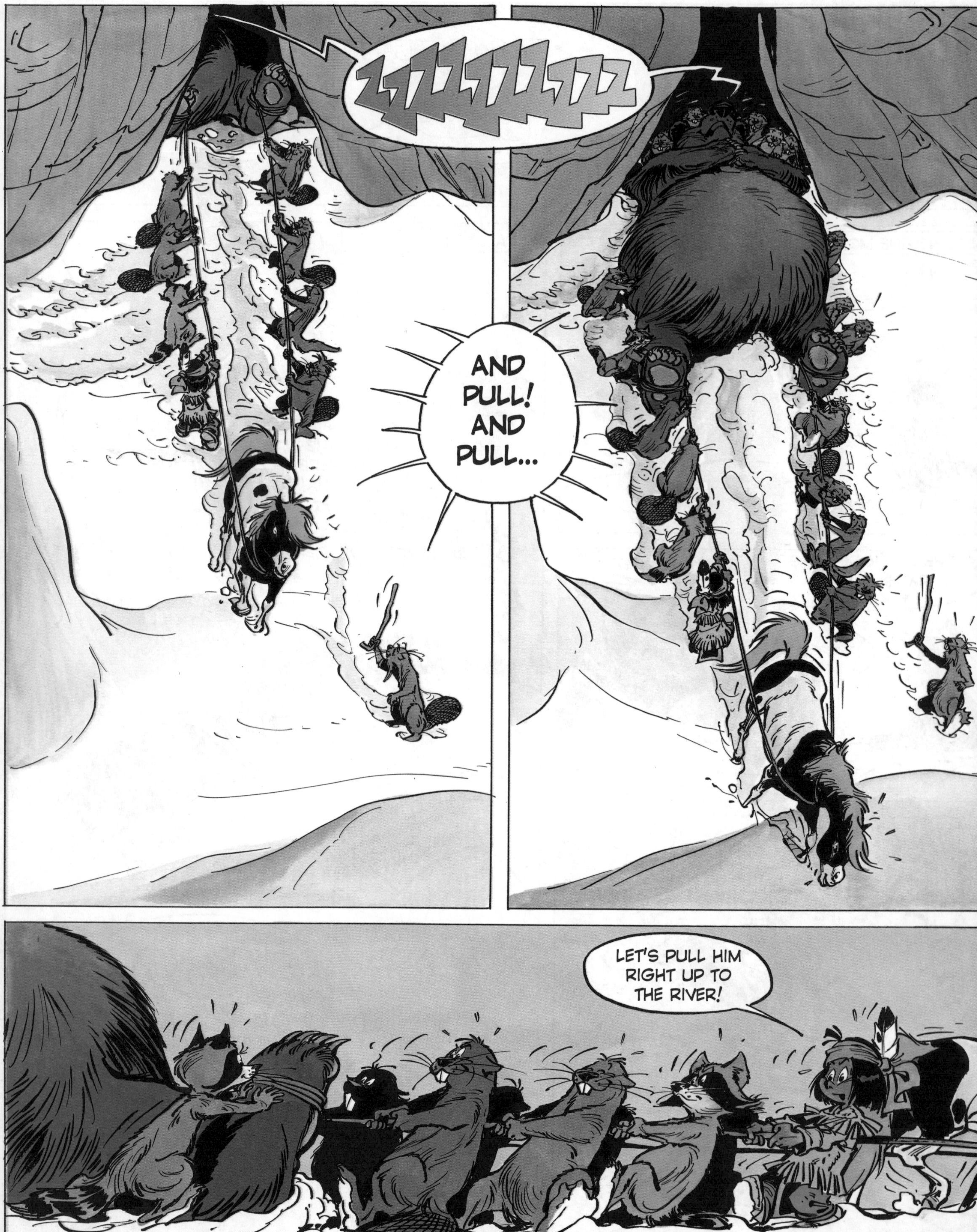
ZZZZZZZZZZZ
AND PULL! AND PULL...
LET'S PULL HIM RIGHT UP TO THE RIVER!

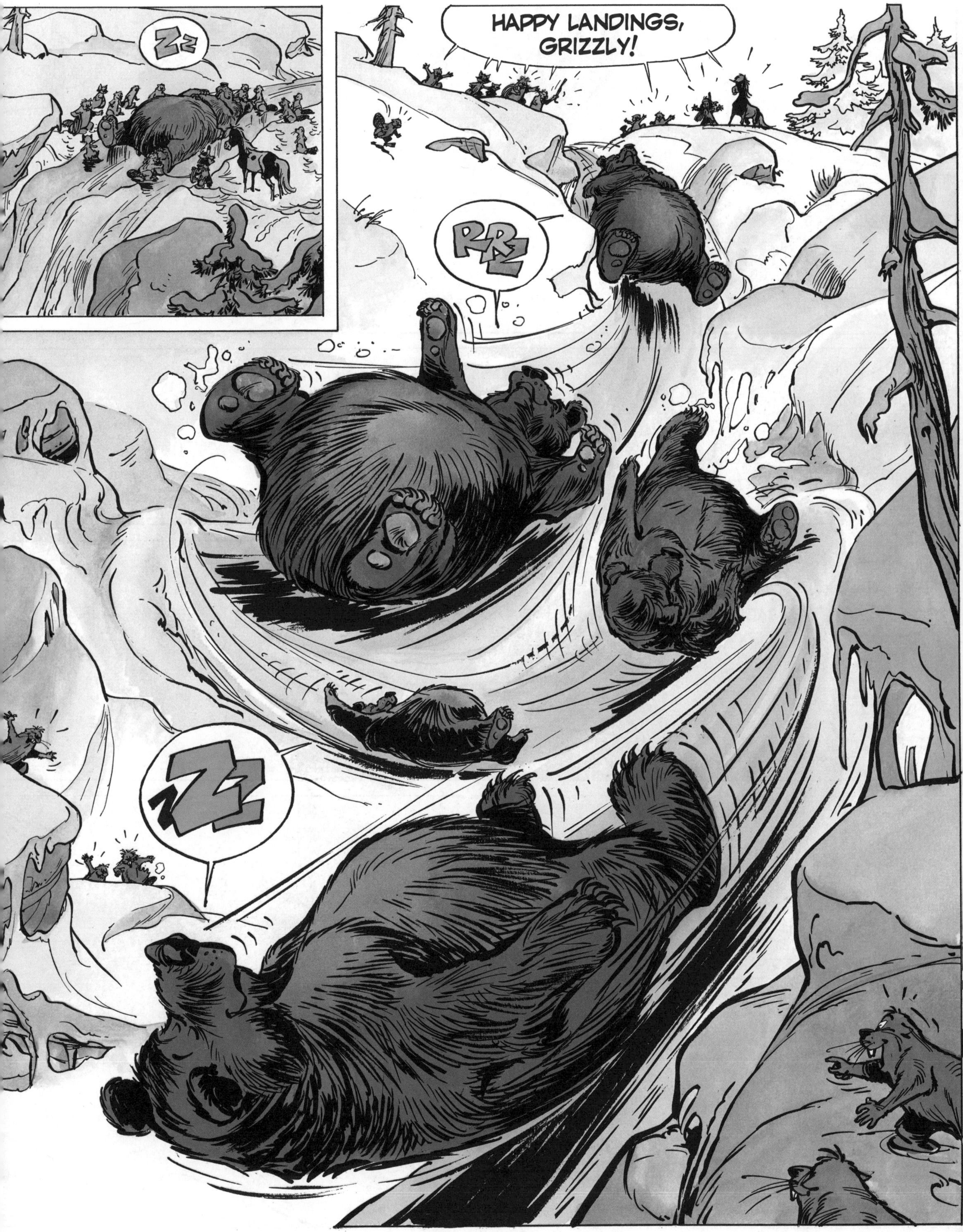
ZZ
HAPPY LANDINGS, GRIZZLY!
RRZ
ZZZ

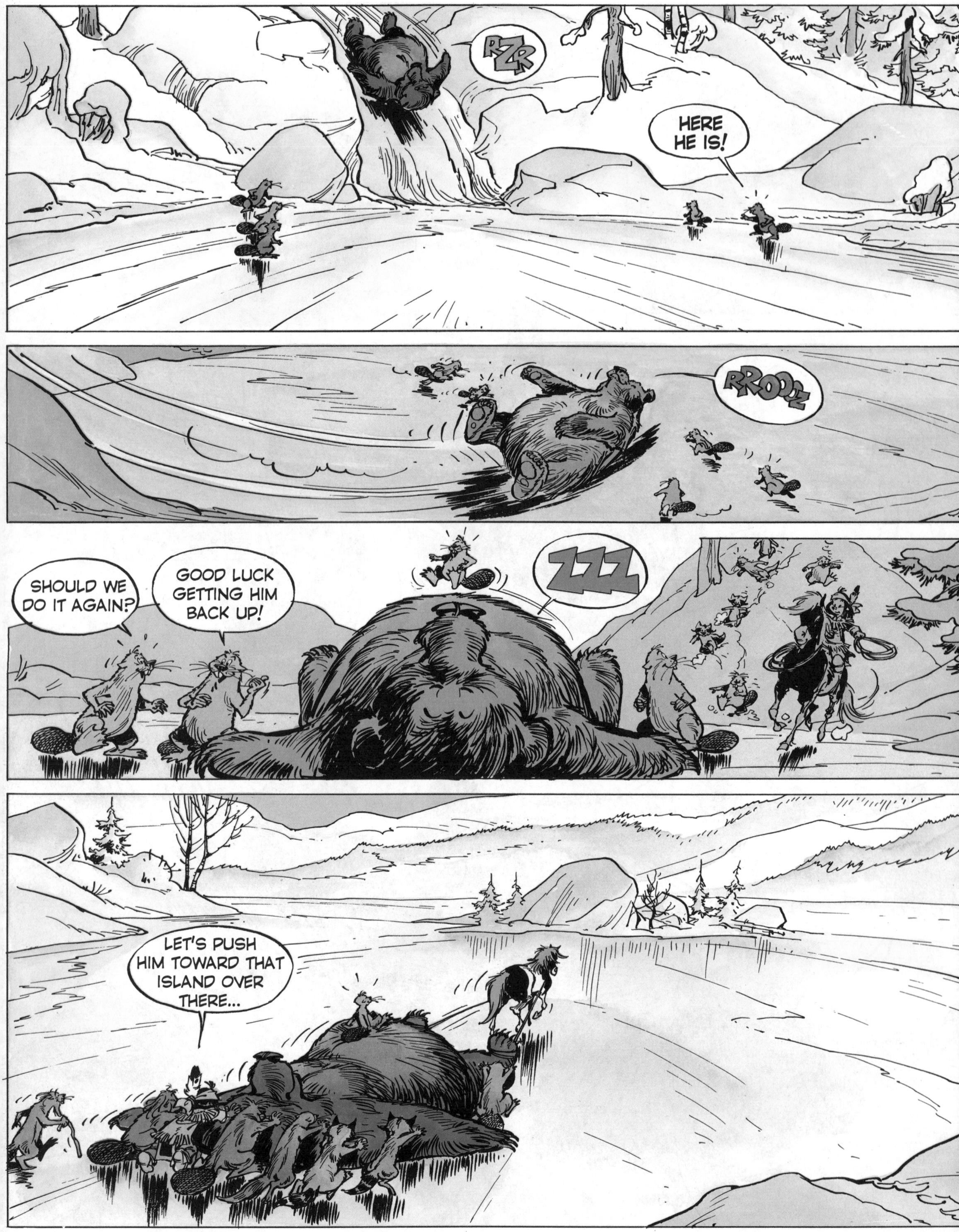
RZR
HERE HE IS!
RROOZ
SHOULD WE DO IT AGAIN?
GOOD LUCK GETTING HIM BACK UP!
ZZZ
LET'S PUSH HIM TOWARD THAT ISLAND OVER THERE...

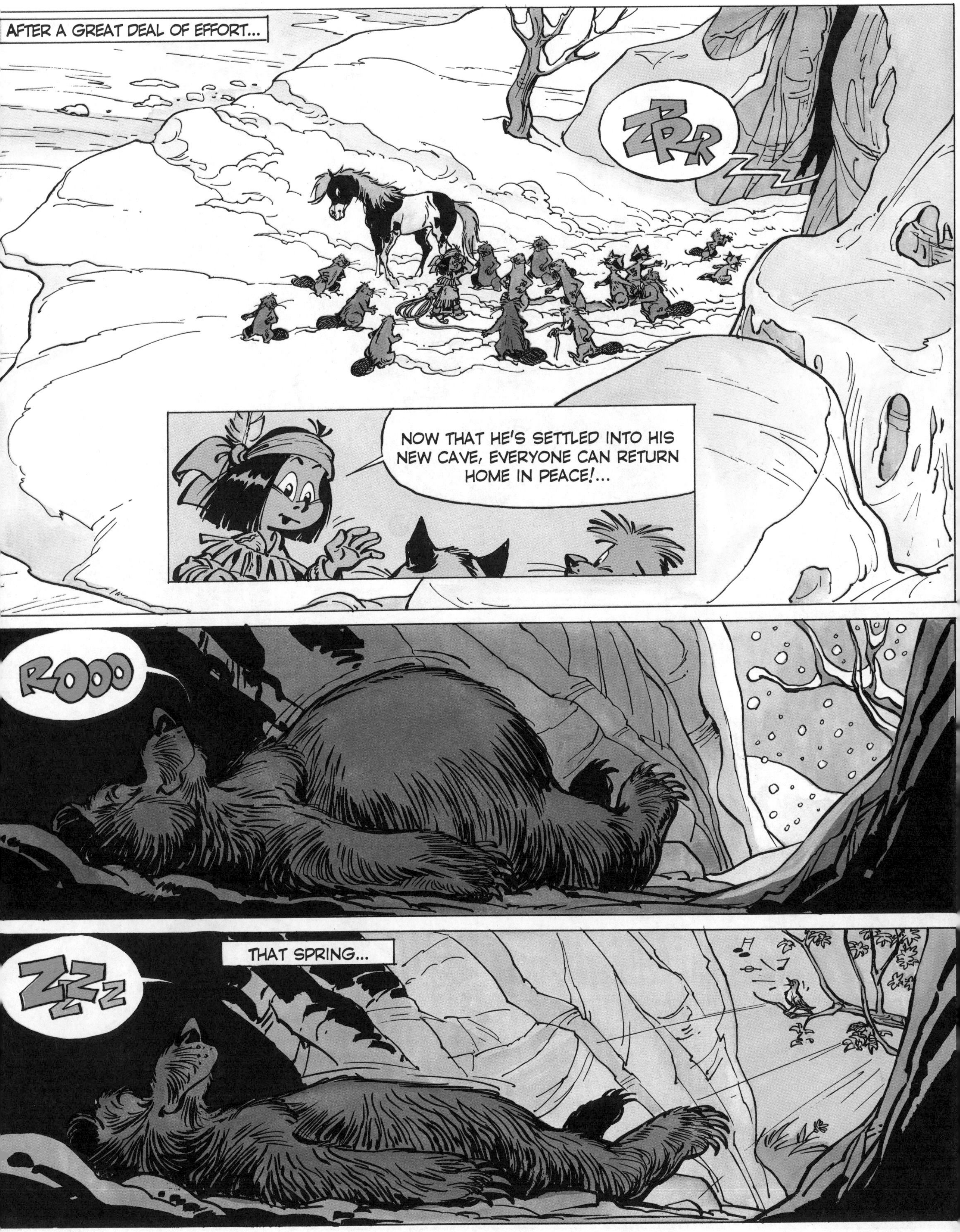

AFTER A GREAT DEAL OF EFFORT...
ZZRR
NOW THAT HE'S SETTLED INTO HIS NEW CAVE, EVERYONE CAN RETURN HOME IN PEACE!...
ROOO
ZZZZ
THAT SPRING...

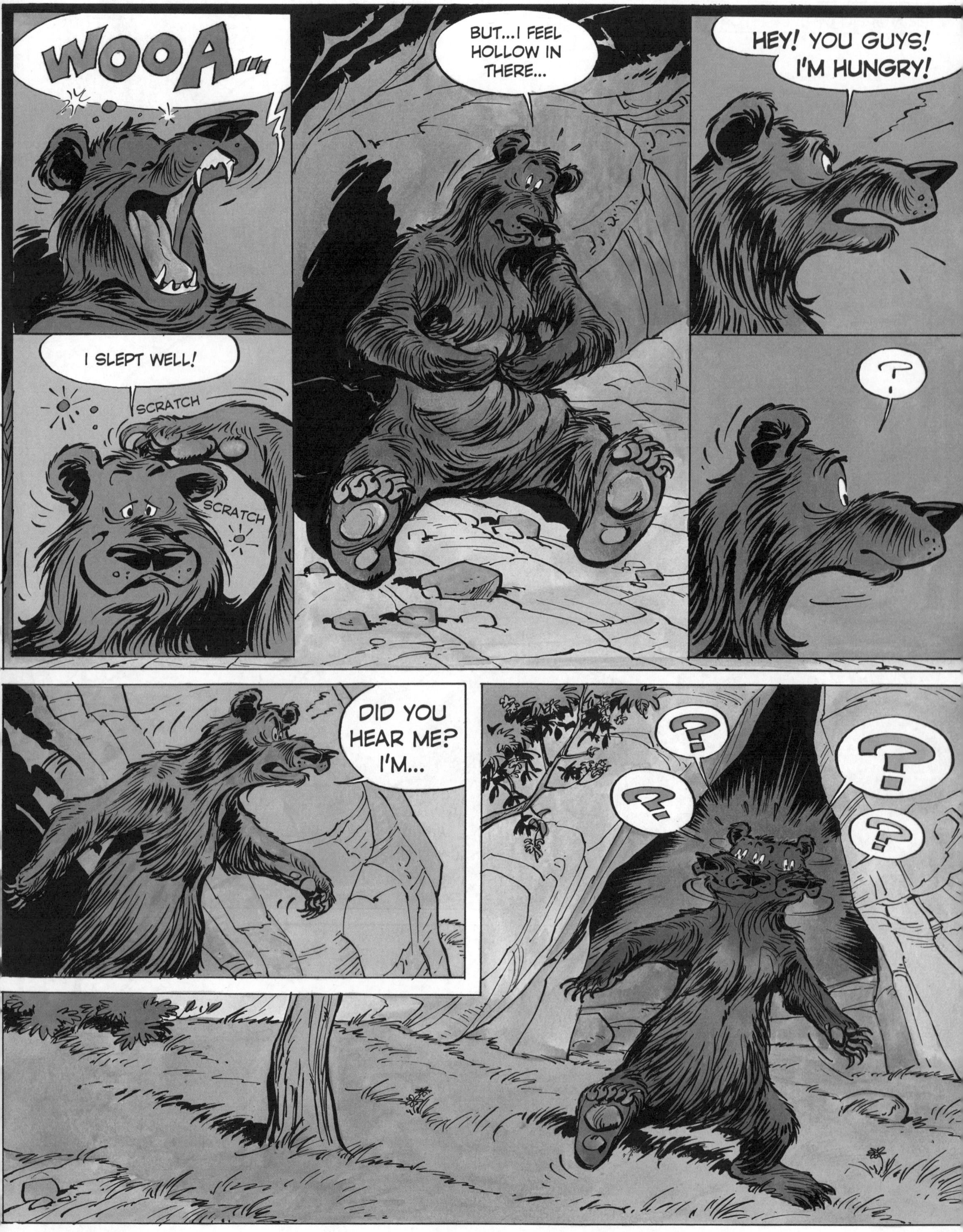
WOOA...
BUT...I FEEL HOLLOW IN THERE...
HEY! YOU GUYS! I'M HUNGRY!
I SLEPT WELL!
SCRATCH
SCRATCH
?
DID YOU HEAR ME? I'M...
?
?
?
?

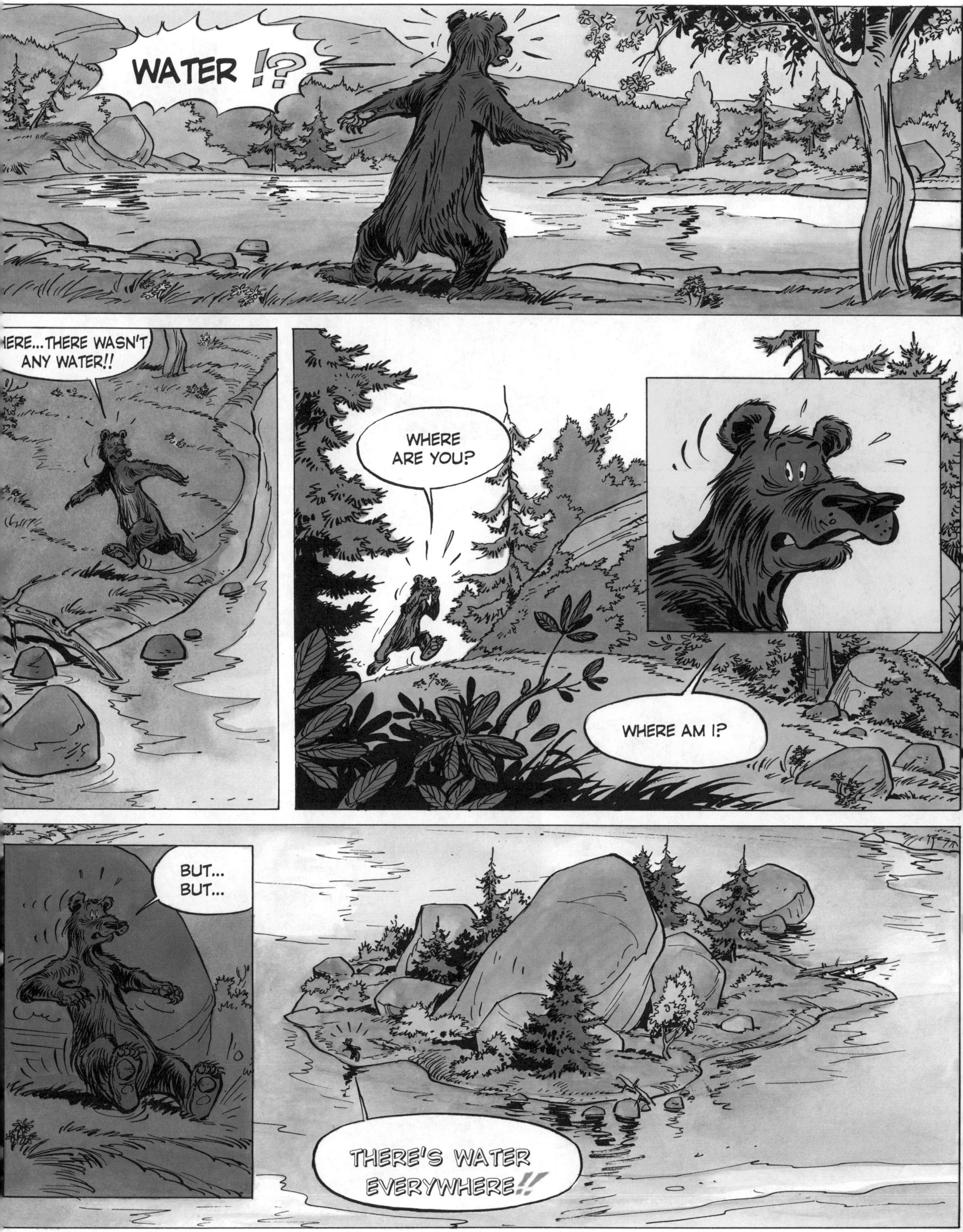
WATER !?
...ERE...THERE WASN'T ANY WATER!!
WHERE ARE YOU?
WHERE AM I?
BUT... BUT...
THERE'S WATER EVERYWHERE!!

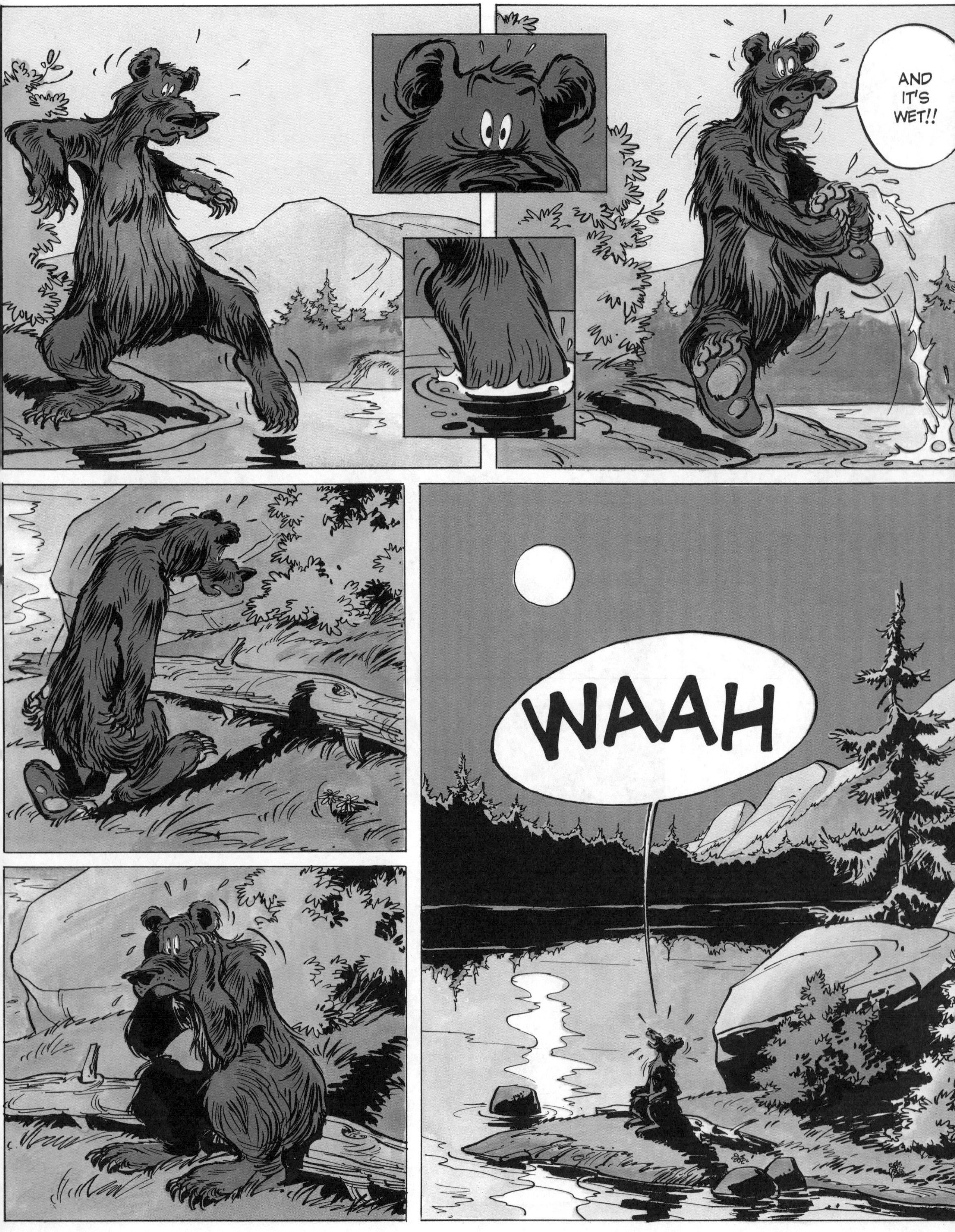
AND IT'S WET!!
WAAH

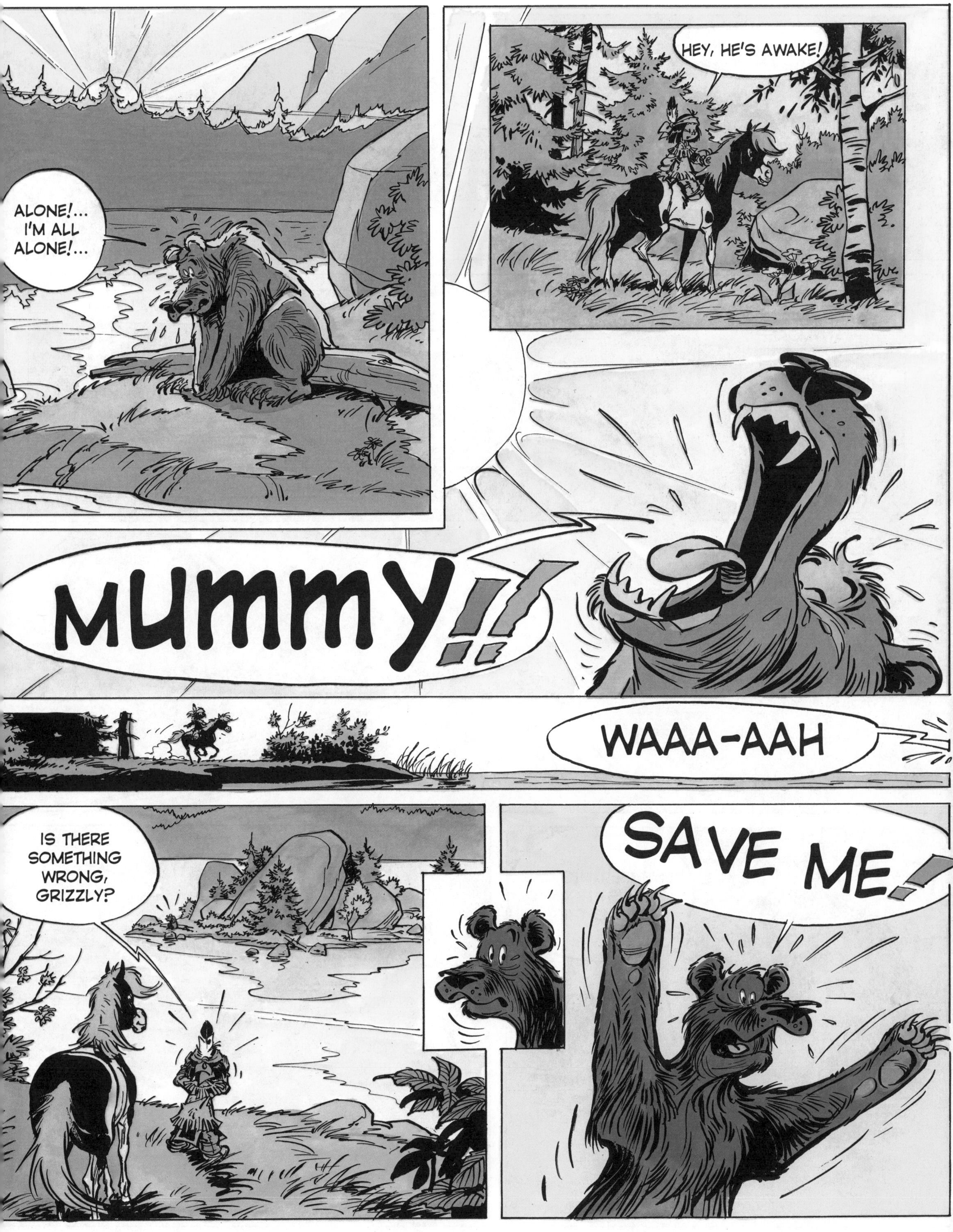
ALONE!... I'M ALL ALONE!...
HEY, HE'S AWAKE!
MUMMY!!
WAAA-AAH
IS THERE SOMETHING WRONG, GRIZZLY?
SAVE ME!

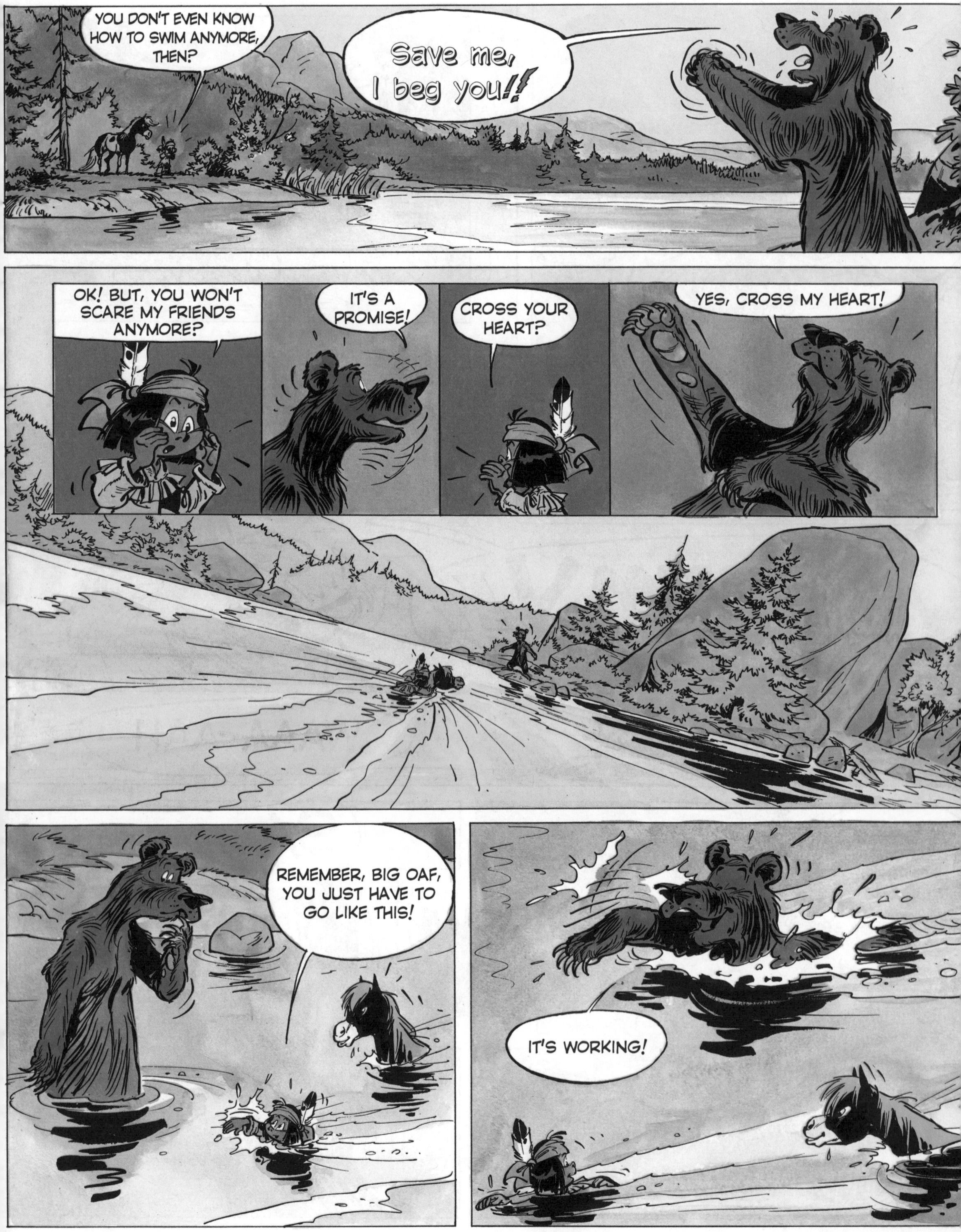

YOU DON'T EVEN KNOW HOW TO SWIM ANYMORE, THEN?
Save me, I beg you!!
OK! BUT, YOU WON'T SCARE MY FRIENDS ANYMORE?
IT'S A PROMISE!
CROSS YOUR HEART?
YES, CROSS MY HEART!
REMEMBER, BIG OAF, YOU JUST HAVE TO GO LIKE THIS!
IT'S WORKING!

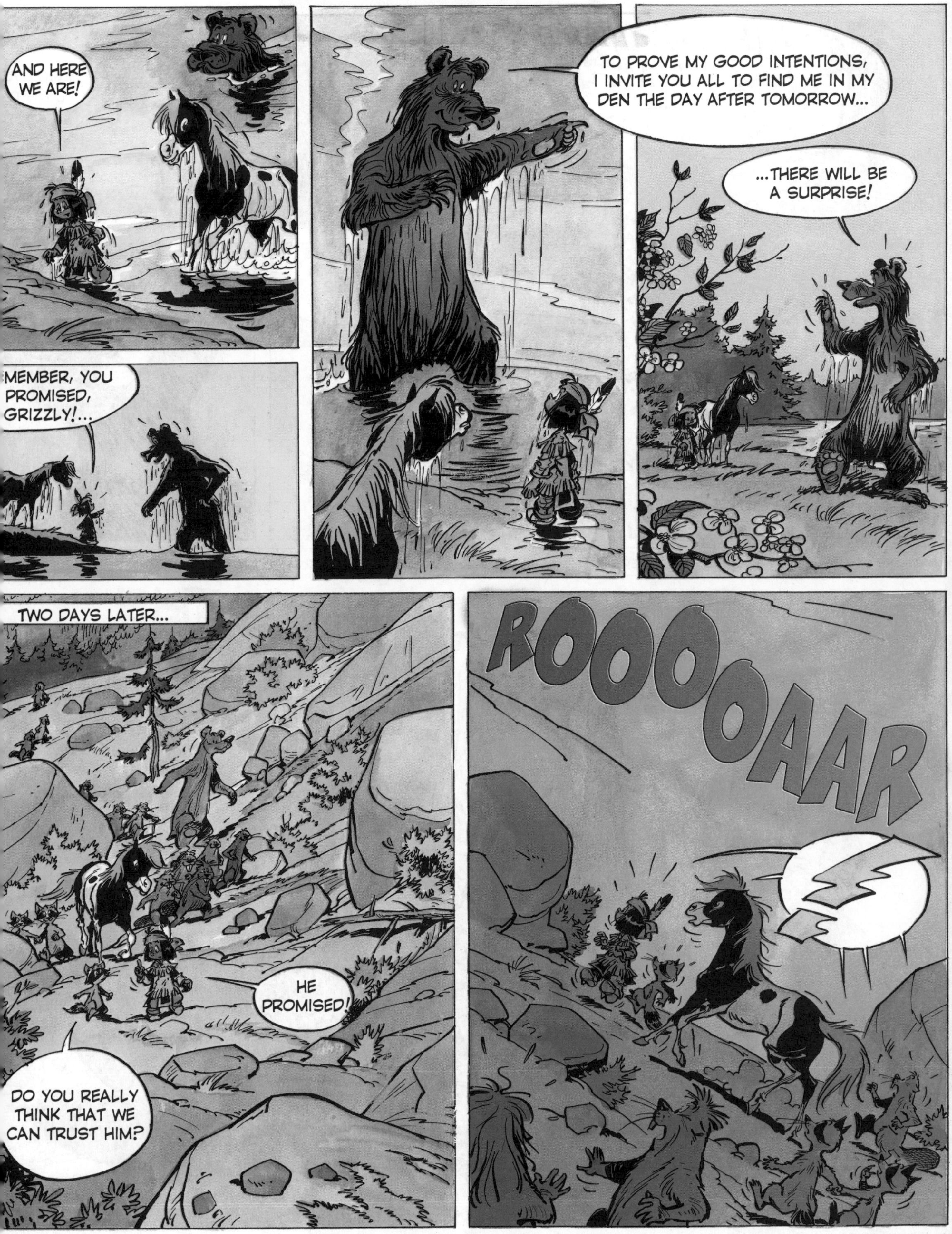

AND HERE WE ARE!
MEMBER, YOU PROMISED, GRIZZLY!...
TO PROVE MY GOOD INTENTIONS, I INVITE YOU ALL TO FIND ME IN MY DEN THE DAY AFTER TOMORROW...
...THERE WILL BE A SURPRISE!
TWO DAYS LATER...
HE PROMISED!
DO YOU REALLY THINK THAT WE CAN TRUST HIM?
ROOOOOAAR

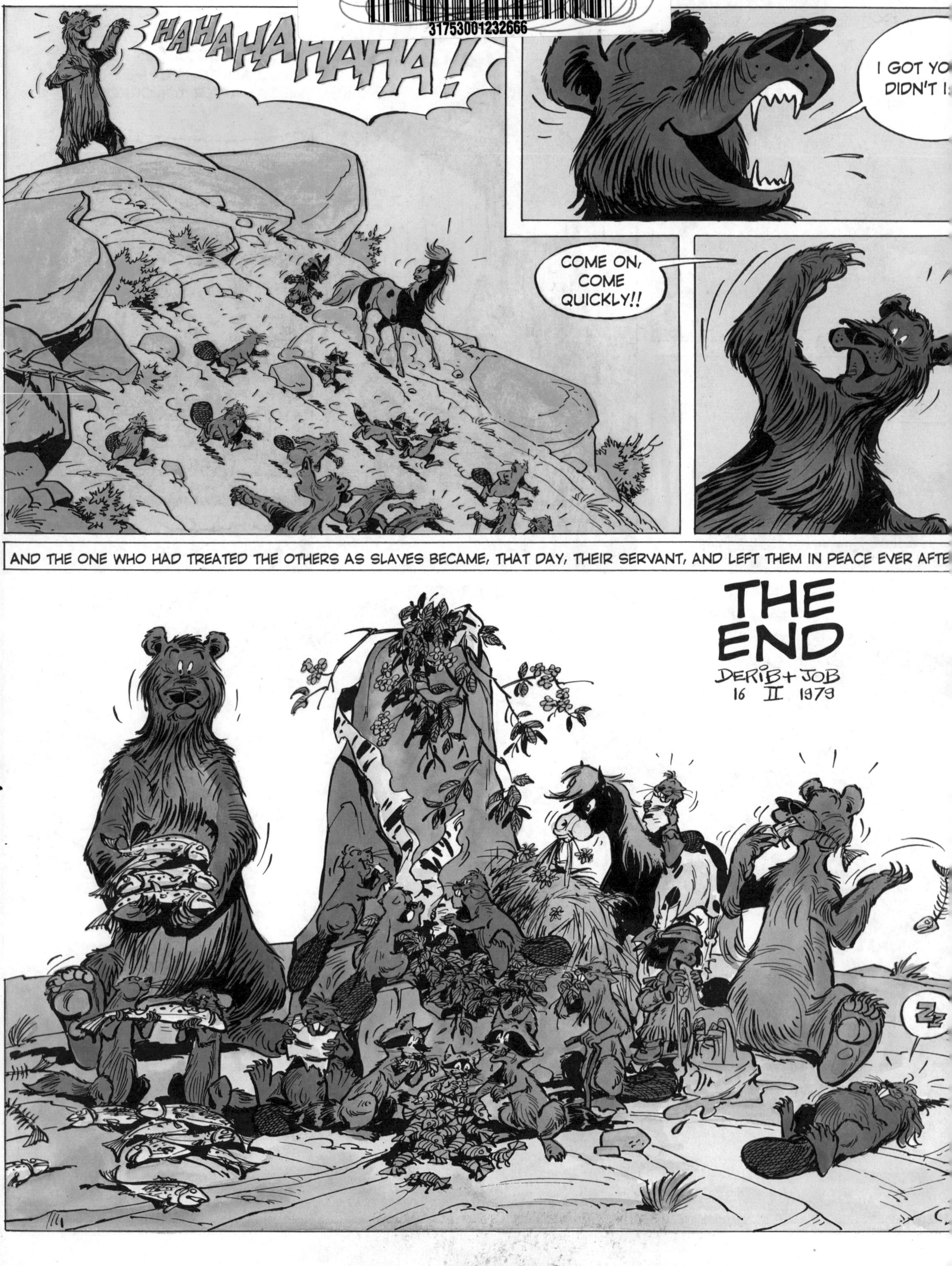
HAHAHAHAHAHA!
I GOT YO
DIDN'T I
COME ON, COME QUICKLY!!
AND THE ONE WHO HAD TREATED THE OTHERS AS SLAVES BECAME, THAT DAY, THEIR SERVANT, AND LEFT THEM IN PEACE EVER AFTE
THE END
DERIB + JOB
16 II 1979
ZZ